the lost coast

the lost coast

STORIES FROM THE SURF

Drew Kampion

ILLUSTRATIONS BY JEFF PETERSEN

Gibbs Smith, Publisher
Salt Lake City

For Alana and Alex
—DK

For my family and Kate Trudi T.
—JP

First Edition
08 07 06 05 04
5 4 3 2 1

Text © 2004 Drew Kampion
Illustrations © 2004 Jeff Petersen

Published by
Gibbs Smith, Publisher
P.O. Box 667
Layton, Utah 84041

Orders: 1.800.748.5439
www.gibbs-smith.com

Designed by Linda Herman, Glyph Publishing Arts, San Francisco
Printed and bound in the United States of America

Library of Congress Cataloging-in-Publication Data
Kampion, Drew.
The lost coast : stories from the surf / Drew Kampion ; illustrations
by Jeff Petersen.– 1st ed.
p. cm.
ISBN 1-58685-214-0
1. Surfers—Fiction. 2. Surfing—Fiction. I. Title.
PS3611.A7556 L67 2004
813'.5—dc22
2003020172

contents

Acknowledgments

Thanks to John Severson, Doug Fiske, Richard Dowdy, John Witzig, David Gilovich, Steve Pezman, Jamie Brisick, Evan Slater, Devon Howard, Alex Dick-Read, and Michael Fordham for publishing my stories, and to Jeff Petersen for the great illustrations, and to Jennifer Grillone for her kind assistance, and to Susan for many cups of perfect coffee.

introduction

THE BEACH IS A NO-MAN'S-LAND, the coastal zone a dynamic give and take of land and sea, swell and tide. The nomadic peoples indigenous to this fluid landscape belong to the global tribe of surfers. They see the ocean differently than inlanders, differently too than the other fringe dwellers who seldom set foot in saltwater.

Surfers read the patterns of the sea like others read a book. For them, the organization of swells, currents, and the curling folds of waves are elements of a natural language, as coherent in structure and meaning as any taught in school.

As energy passing through matter organizes matter, so years of intimacy with the ocean and its waves organizes and alters the perceptions of the surfer. The aura of sprung negative ions, the mathematics of lulls, sets, and rogue waves, the briny stew in which they tumble and struggle, the continual oscillations of reflective surfaces under shifting skies, the lurking presence of The Landlord (a.k.a. The Man in the Gray Suit—sharks) in the murky waters below . . . all of this alters the senses while it educates the surfer, revealing the laws of the universe on a scale that can be engaged and understood.

Here is a collection of surf stories—tales of truth, fiction, and fantasy, most of which have been published over the past thirty years or so—each a glimpse into life on this sweet and ragged wild edge of beauty.

long day

ON A JET-BLACK MORNING in February of 1965, I had just crested the summit, flicked the gearbox into neutral, and was flying down the long, treacherous Oxnard grade. The lights of Ventura, shimmering far off in the distance, were streaked rhythmically by the weathered wiper blades of the coasting 1960 Volkswagen camper van. The 36-horse four-banger idled easily as the wind whistled louder and louder through the seams of the sliding windows. The nose of my 9-foot 6-inch Con surfboard rested on the back of the passenger seat, and the radio had gone to static a few miles back. My right foot was baking under the heat that leaked out of the small front heater tube; my left foot was in Siberia over near the door. I would be in the water at California Street by dawn.

The van swung on its pigeon-toed wheels as it careened faster and faster down towards the Oxnard plateau, where only a few lights twinkled in those days. Oxnard itself was off to the left and sleeping still as I sailed past, once again running in fourth gear, the brass prayer bell tinkling rhythmically with the whump-whump-whump of the highway's oiled seams. On the radio, KRLA suddenly flickered to life with the Four Seasons wailing about Sherry Baby. Ah yes, I knew a Sherry Baby, but that was all behind me now— " . . . tell her . . . everything is all right . . . " and then it was all static again. I fumbled with the dial, but the only stations I could raise were from San Francisco.

There was just enough light under the morning overcast to show me the grim truth about C-Street—small, rainy, and blown out. I cursed and rattled the steering wheel with my fist. I had sacrificed my morning classes at Valley State College and my afternoon hours at the market to be here, and it was crap. I stood in the sandy mud behind the litter of concrete rip-rap and driftwood that formed the beach's berm and sniffed the raw stench of agitated sewage, kelp, and petroleum. The long wooden pier sagged and was dark. Up the point, out past the fairground stables, chocolate lumps of wave dissolved in fitful bursts of whitewater that spanked the ugly shoreline rocks and dissolved into dirty, slow-burning puffs of foam. I would not say I was happy.

I clambered back up into the VW, embarrassingly close to tears, and fondled the wobbling gearshift knob for a second before I twisted the key to start the little engine (whoa-whoa-whoa), then I swung around and headed up the road to the White Bib Restaurant, which was open and already three pots of bad coffee into the dark day.

I took a stool, feeling bleak and disheveled in the face of the waitress's crisp white blouse and pleated black skirt. She poured black coffee into a white cup, but when I looked down I could see right through the liquid to the bottom. I still had time to make it back to the Valley for my second class, and then I could show up for work—tell them I was feeling better now, miraculous recovery. Or I could go further north, check Rincon. It'd probably be a waste of gas, and I was low, but . . .

The Overhead was a dull chaos of shifting peaks and mushy piles of lethargic whitewater—maybe three or four feet, high tide, nothing to ride. Mondos was worse, Stanleys and Hobsons were junk, and the Oil Piers were a sad industrial wasteland in the gray morning. La Conchita Point offered no great hope for Rincon, but I coaxed myself on. Sometimes turning this corner made all the difference. As with other county lines along the coast, the Ventura–Santa Barbara border was a sort of convergence zone—a funky south wind might eddy and swirl and be beautifully smoothed out by the time you got to Rincon.

Rounding the bend and heading along the La Conchita Straight, I could see a little whitewater pushing along the cobbled length of the point a couple of miles ahead. The beachbreak to my left below the highway was glassy but unremarkable with some rideable peaks. I began to hope that Rincon could be fun.

When I got there, six or seven cars were parked along the roadside. A couple of guys were heading down over the boulders with their boards as I U-turned on the highway and pulled over at the front of the row. The waves looked marginal—sectioning two-footers breaking close to shore—maybe a dozen guys out, scattered from creek to cove, dark shapes undulating with the waves. A light gray ribbon of smoke wandered up from a driftwood fire; there was a flicker of flame. Yellow light warmed the windows of a few of the houses nestled in the trees along the point; people were getting ready for work or school.

I leaned back against the van and considered. The air was chill and damp, the waves unpromising, but I was here. The eventual outcome of a series of expectations and justifications had brought me to this inevitable moment. I began to shiver, muscles suddenly contracting with the decision to paddle out.

Lifted the back hatch. Slid out the board. Balanced it across tops of fog-wet granite boulders. Took out a White Stag wetsuit, stiff as cardboard in the back of the van where heat never reaches. Pulled off shoes, let blue jeans drop, slid the cold rubber up over quivering thighs. Frigid neoprene embrace briefly took breath away as I pulled off sweatshirt and T-shirt, thrust arms into short sleeves, squirmed wetsuit up over shoulders. In a few seconds stopped shaking, bundled clothes away, took out quarter bar Parawax, crouched over my stick. Fingers cold, board cold, wax cold and hard—not much transferred rubbing in rumbling circles over the deck.

Slipped piece of wax up wetsuit leg, gathered surfboard under arm, climbed down rocks onto sand, medium tide, 40-degree air, 54-degree water, 8 a.m. Wet sand warmer than the rocks, the first surge of whitewater up legs a shock, but then felt fine. Same with first roll under a wave—cold flush, physical alarm, then fine.

Glassy. Ocean all grays except black wetsuits of surfers, white bursts of foam. Oily smooth in places, then riffled with texture. Suck of each wave exposing sinews of energy drawing forewaters smooth. Rotating peeling plunge over rocky shallows, bending towards me.

Sections curled and burst in several places. Very peaky Rincon. The dozen surfers seemed more like half. Watching, paddling, past first peak. Sat up on shoulder of second, watched beautiful drop, bottom turn into pitching lip. Three-footer swatted board away with surprising speed. Surfer—Gary Brown I recognized—rose cursing, groped over rocks after it, could hear the bump and crunch. Watching, could feel his pain, but next wave—smooth dark slope, completely virgin—gasp of pleasure and seven fast strokes—slide and swoosh into soft saddle of energy, closing on far side, into relaxation. Slipped over the back, resumed paddling, out to third peak, still inside creek mouth, dark gray reflections in windows of unlit beach homes, three surfers walking up the beach.

Then three of us at third peak, more size again, maybe four-foot peaks. Still more size at Indicator, and no one out. Maybe later. Work in gradually.

Nice set coming. One, two—the third mine, alone and uncontested, clean black peak bulging past towards the cove as I dropped in. Fin vibration off the bottom, walling down the line, chance to make bowl section, crouch and crumble, lip of wave in the head, tumbling, board gone, chill turbulence sweeping me bumping over rocks, hands groping protection and purchase, head up to breathe, looking for board, already nested in kelpy rock canyon amidst receding surge of foam and stream. Fortunate lie, but found a crunching ding in the center far rail, ridge of torn fiberglass.

Miracle! Chunk of wax still up my leg. Rubbed it into the gash, sealing and keeping me from scratches, lifting the board over whitewater surges, stumbling for balance, sliding on and paddling out into a lull.

Three guys on the beach, standing at the creek—trunks, no wetsuits—laughing as they waded in, splashing dives out with their boards, yelling it's like bathwater—so warm! Told me they're from Santa Cruz. "We don't wear wetsuits when we come down here," the one named Joe said.

The third peak with six of us for a few sets, then the three Santa Cruzers paddled out to Indicator, and one of the other two disappeared. Two of us to ourselves, tide rising, fattening the waves, shortening the ride.

I kicked out of a wave, paddled to the next peak inside, found a couple more discreet peaks working now, getting mushier, smaller. Finally caught one to the tail-end beachbreak curling across the small strip of sand right below the van. Thought about getting out, going into Carpinteria, something to eat, gas up, see if it got better later. Looking for a wave to take in, a nice wall moved in—snagged it, curling and zippering, crouching, it looped over my head. Kicked out, energized, started paddling back for more. Another little set—not peaky but small, peeling across to the rip-rap seawall—clean and fast, no one else, they're all outside or leaving—and I hold a cheater five (one foot over the nose of the board) for a good twenty-five yards, bury the nose, pull through the back as the shorebreak collapses.

Just a few surfers left, maybe six, as late-morning surge of southeast wind was scuffing it up even worse, but almost at my back as I paddled back out, past the first to the second peak. Tide high, chop and backwash ugly, take-offs became floppy, faces lumpy, waves short. It was time to head in, and me not alone thinking this as the water cleared out in less than half an hour, except for the three Santa Cruz guys barely visible every once in a while through the glare out at Indicator. Standing in the shallows after losing my board in the end section, I waved to Gary as he tied down the trunk of his '64 GTO, his board sticking out fin-up, and tore off—full-throated roar—heading back for his three-to-midnight shift at the market.

It would have been a good time for me to go, too, but the sun was out now, my back was warming towards hot under the wetsuit, and there were waves—not great waves—but rideable waves, at Rincon, with nobody out. Started paddling, bumpy, nose of board slapping down, water splashing my face, squinting into low winter sun, searching for clean wave. Nothing. Sitting, popping kelp bulbs, voices drifting out to me—the three Northern guys heading back down the beach. One of them waved—I was not far off the beach—saying, "It's all yours!" and then it was.

Fog haze eclipsed Channel Islands, but two oil platforms dimly visible. Sun above now and towards straw-colored coastal hills. Few vehicles on Coast Highway as Santa Cruz guys pulled away in old woody, leaving my van alone on roadside, except for a couple cars parked way down along La Conchita beach-break. Hungry again, but warmer too, waiting, one more wave, smell of sun-warmed neoprene.

There weren't many waves, just enough. Each time I rode and paddled back out, another would come in a minute or two. Resolved to surf until after-school crowd showed, then get food, gas, head home. See my girlfriend, go somewhere dark and private.

Then a wave came, long nose time, fast little pockets, standing island pull-out in shorebreak, stoked, reinvigorated, paddling stronger than earlier in the cold and gray. Felt like summer almost. Air crisp and clean in nostrils, hair dry-ing, powdery salt tracings on shoulders, feet stirring figure eights underwater, keeping nose of board pointed towards Indicator, waiting for next wave, which came, again and again, and no one came after school, sun getting lower and lower, haze finally burning off, Channel Islands revealed, tide dropping, swell lines darkening again and back-lit, sections linking, waves lengthening, blue shadows stretching, peeing in wetsuit, goose bumps and late afternoon chill, thinking I should be going, but one more wave, and another, and another.

In the end, water purple and orange, sun dropping behind Santa Rosa Island, tide so low acres of rock and tidepool exposed, blue-black shadows and gleaming patches of reflection, two-foot waves curling snappily around the arc of cobble— wave after wave—arms limp, aching, fatigued, shivering—oily glass and folding pour of lip—two or three halfway strokes to catch one, barely able to push up, stagger to standing, fall backwards into churning surge, careless of direction, rolling over rock and sand. Lifted the board by the tail, tucked it under an arm, breathing hard, watched the last edge of sun evaporate into distant ridgeline, looked in to van, dim glow of daylight still on it, twenty feet above sea level.

I was almost on my way in, but a blue-black set came cracking along, another right behind it, and another. Heaved a groaning sigh, a Shakespearean "tempt me not," and almost wept to hear my mind decide, "One more." Walked out along the low-tide edge, towards dying light, sliver of moon revealed chasing after vanished sun, Venus bright between them, Saturn and Jupiter peaking out of half-night space above, just a thousand-year drive in my van away.

Out near the take-off zone — standing a hundred yards seaward of the stream mouth, lights flickering down at La Conchita Point — houses on the Rincon glowing gold, highway busy with after-work headlights — wading in for yet one more, which obligingly and silently emerged, cracked open on my left as I dropped in, turned, felt it chase me, catch me, chase me all down the weird, low-tide shoreline, finally closing on a small strip of sandbar, leaving me to paw painfully to the beach over barnacled rock in the dark, seeking the bliss of smooth sand, which — when I finally reached it — was burning cold with the deepening night.

A little after 6 p.m., toweling off, side doors opened, sitting there, wiping grit off numb feet with numb fingers, cold air, occasional warm blast from semitrucks rocking the van as they passed, waves almost invisible far out over low-tide reefs, rind of moon lowering towards island — board stowed, wetsuit rolled in towel, last chip of wax flung into the rip-rap, warmer but stiff in jeans and sweatshirt, nose running saltwater, I closed up the back doors and climbed into the front seat.

A couple of arthritic turns and the little engine caught, snorted to life — windows greasy with saltwater and diesel grime smeared into opacity by wipers, cleared enough in a minute to make a cautious U-turn and head north a couple of exits to Carpinteria. Got off and pulled into the Gulf station. Put on socks and shoes while the kid pumped 10 gallons regular at 27.7 per, topping it off at $3.00.

Down the block to the end of road, right a quarter mile to Foster's Freeze, glowing bright in the night on the left. At the window, the nice lady who ran the place asked me how it was while her husband grilled two Charburgers and shook the sizzling basket of fries above rampaging oil.

"It was great," I told her, and only then realized my total satisfaction.

Took the day's now-rumpled newspaper off the condiment counter, sat on picnic table, waited, feeling too hungry to eat. But when it came, it was delicious — that unmatchable gooey sauce of theirs running down my wrists as my mouth dove through a tangle of shredded lettuce and tomato into the sweet hot meat of some former cow, crispy fat fries scooping gobs of ketchup, raw effervescent sizzle of Coke down my throat—parched I finally realized—first drink since morning coffee in Ventura.

Spread open the paper, read while I ate. The Black Muslim, Malcolm X, was shot and killed yesterday by three Black Muslims in New York City. For some reason this felt ominous. And then a few pages into the first section, a small story—President Lyndon Johnson had ordered the bombing of North Vietnamese "positions" in retaliation for last month's Vietcong attack on Pleiku, when eight Americans were killed and over a hundred wounded. I felt a brief twinge of awareness that my Selective Service registration card was in the wallet in my pocket. The II-S student deferment seemed suddenly tenuous. In a nearby story, Defense Secretary Robert McNamara was calling for a nationwide system of bomb shelters. I mopped up the last of the ketchup with the last fry and folded the paper closed.

Later, starting south, swooping down around the Rincon curve, lights of oil piers in the near distance, the point a dim smudge of black, the future crowded around me, whistling with the wind, as I fled towards my girlfriend in the Valley. "Can't forget," I said out loud. "Gotta get that ding fixed tomorrow."

This story originally appeared in the March/April 2001 issue of LongBoard *magazine.*

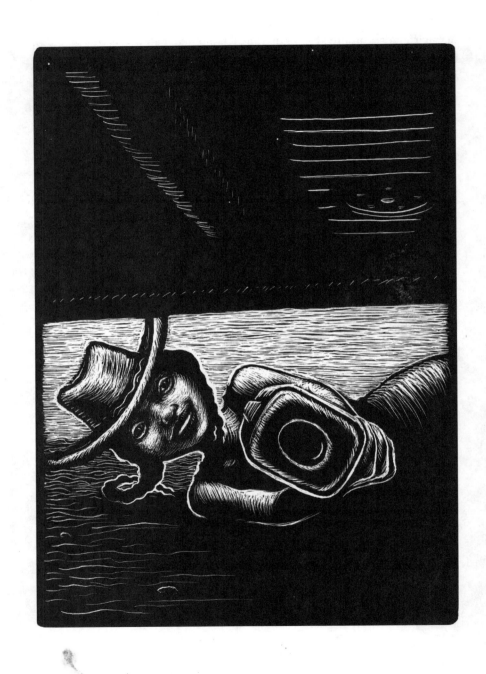

mexico

IT WAS IN THE SPRING OF '75. I was lying in mud, grease, and oil trying to jury-rig a new rubber boot to hold the fluid in the transaxle of my VW van when a piece of cool steel pushed up against my head.

"Hey!" Surprised and irritated, I pulled away and looked at the object and saw there was a hole bored down the center of it, and the hole was pointed at me. A grinning Mexican was lying in the road looking down the barrel of a pistol. She was beautiful.

"Stay there," she said in perfect English, and I froze—with the steady drip of transmission fluid on my forehead. I could feel the van shifting around above me. I heard some thumps and rips and a couple of bangs, and then there was the unmistakable creak of the driver's door and two big feet hit the ground and started towards the señorita. I could see he was wearing nice new huarache sandals—mine.

"Not much," said a north-of-the-border voice. "Couple hundred bucks, credit cards, pretty decent flashlight, but really nice tools—vice grips, screwdrivers, socket set . . ."

He set my toolbox down in the road (not a car had gone by in the whole time I'd been parked there) and started rummaging through it. "Hey," he said after a while. "There's no drive for the sockets. Ask him where the drive is."

"Where's the drive for the sockets?" asked the lovely señorita.

"Uh, it's r-r-right here in m-m-my hand," I answered, experiencing some major constriction in my throat chakra.

"It's in his hand," she told the guy.

"Tell him to throw it out here in the road." His voice was so familiar, so much like any of a hundred guys back home.

"Throw it out in the road," she relayed, and I slid the thing (along with a 13mm socket) towards the guy's feet. When he picked it up I saw he was wearing one of those new Japanese waterproof watches and a woven hippie-style bracelet. He dropped the drive into the toolbox and shut it.

"Let's go," he said.

"Should I shoot him?" asked the señorita, never taking her beautiful eyes off me, smiling until he said, "Yeah," and then, "Nah! Just tell him to stay put for twenty minutes or else then we'll shoot him. Let's went!"

"Stay here," she said and pursed her lips into a succulent kiss . . . and then she was gone. They ran off down the road in the direction I'd been heading. I back-crawled cautiously and looked out around the tire. He had short hair and wore surf trunks, and he was carrying my new surfboard, personally shaped for me by Mr. Reno Abellira in his Sunset Beach shop.

They had parked their car (a powder-blue bug) a hundred yards down the road. I watched them until they got into it, U-turned, and tore off towards Puerto Escondido.

It hadn't been a regulation twenty minutes, but who was to know? The big question was, would the van make it to town before the transaxle froze up and left me with an even bigger problem? I couldn't see that I had much of a choice, so I pulled myself out, got to my feet, pulled that muddy T-shirt off my back, wiped the grease off my head, jumped in and floored it.

I was very attached to my tools. I could take care of anything my van needed; without them I was just another stranger in a strange land. They didn't get all my money—I had little rolls stashed all over—but I needed my tools back.

I followed them at a discreet distance. I didn't pull around a bend until they were disappearing around the next. Maybe 25 miles south of Puerto, I came around a curve, and they were gone—disappeared. I proceeded cautiously. Even so, I almost missed the cut on the left—a muddy little track that plunged into a belt of jungle and down alongside a meandering river. I saw wet tire tracks coming out of the water-filled holes that pockmarked the road—easy to follow.

I camo'd the front of the van with a few viny branches and went for it. When the road forked (five or six times), I followed the tracks. But the closer I got to the coast, the drier it was, so I spent some time studying tread patterns in the dust. I made a few guesses, and I finally came down around a corner and saw the deep blue sea, a clean six-foot swell, and a dead-end fishing village. The VW was nowhere in sight.

I rolled into town, scattered some chickens, bought a fish and some mangoes. Nobody knew nothin' about a powder-blue V-Dub.

I backtracked—took the other fork, backtracked—took the other fork, and on the third one, this weird little fork that seemed to be going away from the ocean finally wound around and down to it, and there they were. A perfect point wave wrapping into a beautiful little cove—golden sand held in the arms of two black spurs of rock. It was bitchin'. They had their camp back up against some trees, some coconut palms just beyond. A small stream ran into the bay at the north end of the beach. They were cooking something in a fire ring not far from a lean-to. It was an awfully nice setup, but they had my tools, and that would not stand.

I set up my own camp. There was a low ridgeline around to the south side of the cove. I pulled the van off into the trees with the side doors away from the road and decked the other three sides with greenery. Then I schlepped some stuff up the hill and staked out the camp from the comfort of a grassy spot in the sun.

It was clear why he was here—speaking just for the gringo. The surf was as much as one guy alone (even with a handful of buddies) could handle. It wrapped, it walled out, it curled three-quarters mostly, but there were two hollow top-to-bottom sections, the second longer than the first. It looked damn good to me, I can tell you. The guy was a pretty hot surfer.

He paddled out right after they ate. I could hear my mother's voice going, "Stay out of the water till you've digested—you'll get a cramp," but it didn't seem to bother him. Then she paddled out—the señorita—and that was a bit of a rush. She surfed very, very well; she had the spot wired.

I had the urge to run down and snatch back my stuff, but I had no clue how long they'd surf, where they kept the gun, and so forth. I figured I should watch them for a while—see what the patterns were. I sashimied a piece of fish and ate it with mango. I watched them surf, then come in, then swim in the river for a while. I watched them walk around naked, work on their campsite, and eat. He checked out some things in the car, she hung towels out to dry. I dozed off.

Next day the surf was even better. It was pushing eight-foot Hawai'ian, and the whole thing was cracking top to bottom—an intense hundred-yard ride. The señorita stood near the mouth of the stream, spearfishing. She was a goddess.

Now or never. I circled around and checked out the car (no pistol, no tools), then slipped into camp. I found my wallet, the good flashlight, and my tool kit in a cardboard box under a blue tarp with other spoils of the highwayman's trade. Then I heard the guy scream from the water. At first I thought he was yelling at me, but he'd just cut out of a smoking barrel and was celebrating. I watched him paddle back out and catch another. I wanted to paddle out there real bad. I was wondering what I could take that would make up for the Abellira, the money, and the inconvenience. I was considering my options when I heard the hammer of the gun click.

"Señorita," I said, reflexively giving her a sort of bow. She was smiling, so I told her why I needed my things and what I was doing in Mexico and where I was going . . . when I got going. I told her I'd really like my money back, if they could spare it, and then the hammer of the gun clicked again.

I'm not saying I'm good-looking—I've never been much of a lady's man—but she came with me. Her name's Maria—can you believe it?—and we've been together ever since. As for Nick (that was his name), he went on to become a successful oil painter, but he died about five years ago—took a fin in the head from that Reno Abellira board. Bad karma.

A couple of years ago, Maria and I came back to the cove. The place hadn't changed—still deserted, still reelin'—and we never left. Speaking of which, I gotta go. Maria's out there all alone. Can't have that.

This story originally appeared in the June 2000 issue of Surfing *magazine.*

to experience surfing

I FELT AN ODD SENSATION even before I saw it. My father and mother were in the front seat, and I was in the back with my sister. We had just moved to California from the Midwest. Everything seemed strange and new to me, and I had been avidly taking in all the new impressions along the way. But then quite suddenly, as we neared the crest of a long hill, everything changed. Things became vividly familiar, and I began to feel almost nostalgic. I knew I had been here before, and it didn't seem that it had been so long ago.

A few flashes swept through my mind—extremely emotional—they seemed to be memories of dreams I'd had when I was still quite young. I was feeling confused, almost panicky, as we passed over the crest of the hill and started down the other side. And then I saw it—the huge, even horizon, the ocean of blue. Just at that moment, as I was seeing it for the first time, a car roared by us down the hill. Though I had never seen them before, I knew immediately that the beautiful, sleek shapes tied to the roof were surfboards. My heart leapt, and I grew quite agitated.

"Look!" I shouted to my family. "Those are surfboards!"

"Where?" cried my sister, leaning forward over the front seat.

"There!" I shouted, pointing at the disappearing car.

My father spoke as if he had seen it all before. "They do a lot of surf riding out here in California," he said. "Most of 'em are just beach bums or kids who are afraid of an honest day's work. Dropouts. Now, over in Hawai'i, that's where you get the really big combers. I remember during the War . . ."

I didn't care what he said; it didn't matter. I felt strongly that at last I'd hooked up with something I'd been waiting for all my life.

My father kept talking while I was in an agony of impatience. He drove so slowly I couldn't stand it! I wanted to be there at the beach to see those guys take the boards off the roof of their car. I wanted to see waves (I only had a vague imag-ination—or was it a memory?—of what they were like). I wanted to see surfing!

"If they can do it, I can do it—but I'm not very good at physical things. Maybe I can't—I probably couldn't—and anyway I'm sure I can't. But, if they can do it . . ."

These worrisome thoughts turned over and over in my head as I carried the old board down near the water's edge, laid it on the wet sand, and began to wax it with a fresh, new bar of paraffin.

It was a gray, overcast day and the ocean was the color of lead. The surface of the water was so smooth and slick that it was like lead too. For all my nerv-ousness, I felt I was almost acting a part—as if I already knew how to do this, how to surf—and I had to find out whether or not I already knew.

The water was colder than I expected, lapping around my ankles, then around my knees. There were other surfers out in the water, gliding across the oily wave faces, paddling on their knees, sitting off beyond the place where the waves broke. It was all so familiar; there was a certain order in it.

I slid up onto the deck of the old board and began to paddle awkwardly. It was hard to keep it moving straight, and then I started leaning the wrong way, and I plunged off into the water. My body seemed to panic with the icy shock; I struggled back aboard.

Eventually I joined the others in the lineup. The ocean was moving with swells that had seemed so small from the shore, but out here they seemed large and ominous. There was so much movement that it was confusing. Waves were moving in, surfers were paddling in different directions, others were sliding down the humps of water, and the waves themselves were spilling and coiling and filling the air with their rushing sound. Someone saw that I was new at this and suggested that I move more forward on my board to keep from pushing water with the nose. Later the same surfer showed me how to turn the board around by circling my legs in the water. He told me to wait till the wave looked like it was just about to break and then paddle as hard as I could towards shore. I tried this several times, drove the nose down under the surface on each occa-sion, and made several long swims to the beach.

I was numb with the cold and exhausted from the swimming. I felt dis-heartened and embarrassed. I sat bobbing in the lineup feeling a familiar emotion that all through my life had preceded "giving up."

But a wave rose up outside and the surfer who had helped me hollered "paddle!" so I paddled as hard as I could towards shore, felt the wave pass under and lift me, saw that my nose was still above the surface, and felt a rush of speed. I struggled to my feet; the board chattered across the surface; the wind whistled in my ears. This was it! I remembered!

After two winters of sticking it out through the coldest weather and the gnarliest swells, I came to think of it as "My Spot." It didn't break so well in the summers, so we went elsewhere, usually south. The water was warmer south, and that was nice, but it was never quite the same. The crowds were meaner, and there were more kooks, so I looked forward to the fall and the first northwest swells.

We all rode shorter boards now, which was such a treat because they were so light to carry and so loose in the water. And we could do new things with them; we thought we were pushing the "outer limits" when we slapped them off the lips of four-foot waves and roller-coastered over with the whitewater. Or we'd run way out onto the shoulder, carve straight back at the breaking part of the wave, then try to bring it around before it gobbled us.

I remember in particular a November evening; the sun was down, and there were only three of us out. It was one of those lulls that seems to come about that time of day when you want one best wave and it won't come.

Finally there were dark lines outside—a squadron of pelicans heading south skimmed closely over the top of the first wave. Watching them, I had drifted a bit too far south of the reef, so the other two surfers got the first two waves. But the third was mine, and there was the joy of paddling for it with no one else to contend with—just this smooth hump of wave and me.

I slid into it, and it jacked up to about five feet by the time I hit it off the bottom. I jammed up into the lip, came straight back down, then carved hard and shot off towards the shoulder. I carved a deep, hard cutback and came back at the pocket, then wheeled it around and pulled hard off the bottom again. But the tide was lower than I had counted on, and the wave hollowed out ahead of me for about twenty yards. Usually I would have roller-coastered or straightened off, but I knew it was the last wave of the day, so I pulled it up tight under the lip and went for it.

The hollow of the wave was smooth and sucked out. I raced along for longer than I expected, but then the whole lip threw out and over me. I was locked inside, racing along, just waiting to get nailed. I went further and further. The wave was like a tunnel, and I was way back in it. Ahead of me, the darkening sky was an oval framed by the moving water; time seemed to stand still. Then I saw the planet Venus framed in the end of the tunnel, and I raced to make it. It was all clear to me now: Surfing was the thing to do, and this was the place to be.

A *longer version of this story appeared in the August/September 1977 issue of* Surfing *magazine.*

when nothing else matters

A ROOSTER CROWS. You open an eye. Sunlight jabs in. You roll over. A mosquito zings by, banks a turn, and zeroes in. The swat on your cheek does the trick. You rise up, slip on your trunks, and go out onto the porch. The sound of the waves (you have become so used to them, each day) is louder outside. You walk across the dew-wet lawn to the cluster of palms that block the view from your window, and stand there and look out on ten- and twelve-foot Sunset.

Fifteen people are out already, but the waves are consistent, one after the other, so you run around to the side of the house and pull your 8-foot long Brewer out from underneath, take the wax off the window ledge, and head on out to the beach.

The sand is golden and cool. A sweet, light, sudsy flavor is in the air: surf and plumeria and your own emotional energy. Rub the wax in figure eights onto the deck of the red board, stick it in your pocket.

Run down the beach, feet sinking an inch or two, the sand moist and grainy and warm where it is wet with the ocean. You come to the rip, wait for a wave to rush up to the crown of the sand, then run with it as it flows back to the sea. Throw the board down, out ahead of you, and slide onto your belly. Paddle as fast as you can till you are outside of the shorebreak, heaving and crashing and splashing out with the rip.

A quarter mile in three minutes and you are working your way out of the rip and over into the lineup. Some friends are there, wet already, and they greet you with big smiles. The waves are perfect, one says. Another yawps agreement.

Way inside you can see the cars parked on the Kam Highway. A bus just went by, taking the early morning shoppers into Honolulu. On the beach a few figures stoop, looking for puka shells; palm trees are thick at the edge of the sand. You are flushed with the run and the paddle-out, and exhilarated by the water. A slight breeze blows off the pineapple fields, down through the canyons: sweet and winsome.

The guy next to you moves, begins to paddle. You turn and look out to sea. A dark line approaching. A thick, fat hump of water moving soundlessly closer and closer: a bluebird they once called them. You stroke frantically out towards it, praying not to be caught inside where your board would surely be snatched from you and then that terrible swim against the rip . . .

Closer and closer it comes, growing steeper. You and the pack of others, clawing up the face as it fringes whitewater at the top and begins to come over, and your friend turns and strokes down the face at the last instant and is gone — into another world.

Outside is another, larger wave. You paddle hard. Fresher than the others, you pull out ahead, and have time to turn while they are still trying to make it over. You stroke towards the shore. You are lifted, lifted. A deep trough sags low before you. The water descends like a wide slide. You feel it catch you, then hurtle you forward with incredible acceleration. You take the drop coming to your feet.

You drive down and down, carve around a surfer trying to make it over, but you know he will be caught inside and have to swim because the wave is already coming out over your head. You turn hard at the bottom and draw back tight against the wall of the wave and rocket along to your right. You touch a hand to the water surface, and your fingers flap and chatter as if from a speedboat, and when you turn to glance towards the shore, you cannot see it because the wall of water has come out over your head and surrounded you, and there is just a big, fat hole in front of you, and you are going for it and definitely, positively, absolutely nothing else matters.

This is an excerpt from a story that appeared in Surfer Photography *in 1975.*

the first dream

"Once there was a wave to get back home again."
—after the Beatles

FINALLY IT CAME. There was no possible preparation. Everything—the past, relationships, plans, hunger, the future, memories, noble emotions, investments, ideas, all systems and constructions—were immediately and completely irrelevant.

You imagine, you visualize, you wonder: The Big One. Great raw shoulders of tectonic plates rubbing against each other, shaking things up, knocking things down, crushing soft bodies. You imagine the Richter scale as sort of a 1-to-10 thing. You visualize the worst that can happen. You wonder where you will be, where your wife will be and your kids.

But on the beach—flattened simultaneously by an explosion of sound and a blast of movement, the sand itself losing its affinity for gravity, your eardrums shocked out of existence, your body in total spasm and contraction, blood oozing from your pores and fingertips and eyes, the sky quickly vanishing in the noontime eclipse of massing shock waves, the earth itself arching to vertical, the sea rushing trembling cold fingers right up your back, as ancient images fly out from the depths of your memory and fill you with an awakening horror and fear, then certainty, that this has all happened to you before, perhaps again and again before, to you and to the entire living world—you know that it's at least a 15, and you and every other being are going down.

The beach, the point, the pier—seen suddenly from a distance, from above—you experience a brief confusion, not knowing what to look for, then see yourself, down there, where you were sitting beside your surfboard, resting between go-outs, the whole mass turned 45-degrees to the horizon and steepening and lifting, pushing the ocean and its weirdly oscillating wave patterns further and further away, heads bobbing as they're pushed at high velocity towards the west, the shimmering, weedy sea bottom surging up and up and up till you and your board and everyone and all the sand and palm trees and cars and trucks and houses and buildings begin to slide down towards the water. The whole coast, you marvel, exactly like a great sinking ship—passengers, crew, and everything loose sliding down the tilting deck into the gullet of the sea, while wobbling 747s corkscrew down out of the sky.

Yet you are strangely unconcerned, even serene. Your vision is clear though your hearing is still oddly muted—as if you'd stuck your head out of a car window at fifty miles an hour. But there's no wind. And there's no sense of taste either, or smell, or touch. Just pulses, like sound, and the broadening vision of the entire coast now—from Sunset Point and Santa Monica to Point Mugu and Oxnard—broken along the spine of the Santa Monica Mountains and simultaneously lifting and steepening. To the east, beyond the widening fracture, you watch another slab of land torque and sheer, lift and tilt—this one from north of Point Conception down to Baja—and behind it another, even greater earth wave, from Eureka to Bakersfield to Phoenix. The higher you drift, the more you can see. The clarity of your vision is not affected by distance. Your range is enormous now, as if from a satellite, and you can see the crumpling back of the continent shivering in slow motion and clouds of dust and smoke muting the details of its forever-altering surface.

It's like you're in the water, floating, waiting out the passing of the wave that ripped your board towards shore. You roll over onto your back and look up towards the surface, but it's stars (and over to your right the sun) and you feel yourself being lifted towards them exactly as your lungs would start to lift you gently towards the light. And then this space, you notice, has its curve too—subtle, like the air currents that gliders ride—and your attention goes to that. In some way you manage to move up towards that dim curvature, get alongside of it, feel its arcing flow accelerate. You find a line along its movement, at right angles to the flow. You feel a smile as you understand you've found a wave to surf. You are completely at home with it, an essential vector of energy poised precisely for optimum trim on a timeless trip to . . .

The wave gains definition, gathers a sense of mass and density. You understand that this is because of its increasing speed and compression. Subtly, but quite intentionally, you alter your attitude, adjust your stance, and—to your surprise and satisfaction—feel the anticipated bite of acceleration.

The wave has changed color, you notice. It's gone from black to the darkest blue, and it continues to grow lighter, all the while accelerating and compressing until it is a definite bright blue tube and you are screaming through it with the exquisite blend of tension and release that you only get a few times in life. But now it's sustained, and intensifying. And exhilarating. No terror. No unknown. No thoughts. Pure experience.

You're not alone. You suddenly become aware you're sharing this wave. Bright white forms—entities—emerge like droplets from the top of the wave and splash open into identity right before you. Some are familiar—family, friends, surfers from years ago—and some aren't, but you know them anyway. Their energy is warm, welcoming, deeply satisfying. Endlessly they explode into existence, sweep past you and gather in your slipstream, adding their delight to your delight in the most thrilling ride of your life. Your life . . .

The tunnel glows. The blue-white space twists around you like a funnel cloud. There is a light at the end of the tunnel. When you see it you realize that your sliding was really your being pulled, reeled in by the light, a light so intense you are amazed you don't have to squint to look at it . . . growing larger . . . brighter . . . the forms around you now heard, voices in chorus, layers of harmony . . . you and the experience of absolute velocity with just a trace of friction to stroke the residue of sensory appetite . . . and then you surf straight into the light.

And you break through.

Surface. Interface between two surfaces. One is dense and heavy but will assume any shape. The other is thin and light and will also assume any shape. The second can be expanded or compressed. Call the first water and the second air.

Now I remember.

I remember when I was you, and everything that went before you. From the Big One and the Fall and the surfing that you did and the car that you had and the job and the friends and the family and the town and the nation and the world and its history back through all technologies and revolutions and holocausts and societies and wars and migrations and life-forms and lands and evolutions and seismic movements and planetary formations and stellar congealings and galactic pulsations, expanding forever back to and out from that first great explosion, the Big One, the Big Bang, just after the collapse of the eleven-dimension universe, just after . . . Just after . . .

Now I remember.

I am. Alone. I split myself in two. But I continue to watch both halves. I discover the surface between the two. One heavy. One light. Both infinitely changeable. I bring attention to this interface, charge it with my infinite imagination, and set it spinning on itself. A curious thing happens. Set in motion, it returns energy to me. I play with this surface, this interface. I learn to move effortlessly across its surface, drawing in the energy. I feel delight; I sense an appetite. I sense speed, and I focus on getting more. The interface is spinning around me. I am aware of myself. I love this! Look what I've done! I feel pride. I feel a disruption in the interface. Ahead the shape distorts. I hit it at high speed. There is a burst of light—a bang and I explode . . . I am several, then more . . . my awareness multiplies . . . I fly from the center in a thousand directions.

I am lost. I am apart from the rest. Every moment further from the source. Expressing new identities at every level removed—galaxy, star, planet, earth, tree, fish, dolphin, human—and then eating, gathering, hunting, warring, farming, building, fighting, loving, thinking, feeling, creating, teaming, surfing—and then born in Pasadena, moving to Huntington Beach at eleven, learning to surf at twelve, finding the long wall at thirteen and the tube at fourteen, starting out on a search for the perfect wave at eighteen but never finding it, getting a wife, getting a job, having kids, teaching them to surf and seek and never find it too, then surfing one miserable crowded morning at Malibu, coming in to rest from the crowd and the smog and the junk waves, feeling absolutely lost and aimless and alone, when—there's that sound again—the fabric of reality is pulled apart, and I start my long, lovely journey home. What a trip!

I remember. The pride. Then the wipeout.

I begin again. I split myself in two. I continue to watch both halves. I find the surface between the two. One heavy. One light. Both infinitely changeable. I bring attention to this interface, charge it with my infinite imagination, and set it spinning on itself. Set in motion, it returns energy to me. I play with this surface, this interface. I move effortlessly across its surface, drawing in the energy. I feel delight. I sense speed, and I focus on gaining more. The interface is spinning around me. I am aware of myself. Faster and faster. What if I lose it again? What if there's another Bang? I feel fear. I feel a disruption in the interface. Ahead the shape distorts. I approach it at high speed. What, I wonder, will I dream this time?

This story first appeared in the Fall 1992 issue of The Surfer's Journal *vol. 1, no. 3.*

eye sight

SPACE

Imagine the nothing beyond blackness. Out of this nothing, gather the warm blackness of space around you like a blanket.

The Universe!

Splashes of Galaxies staggering off into infinity; white life sustained in the void by what?

You are your eye, imagine, flying through the Universe.

Imagine!

DREAM

We are all together, naked under the sun. We lie in the warm sand, watching long, long waves peel perfectly, scaly bright and shimmering as if in a dream.

SHARED DREAM

Flat again!

Sitting in the water waiting for a set that never came, filth slippery on my wetsuit, and oppressed by the company of every goon from Point Conception to the Mexican border, it was another typical day at the 'Bu.

Where was the bait they fed you about Man And The Sea? Where was all the pineapple and pussy? Where!?

Miraculously a wave came.

Fifty guys turned their boards. A hundred eyes retreated behind sneering lids. Twenty-five dominant-subordinate interchanges ensued.

The wave hissed in until the sound of its approach was buried beneath the churn of paddling, the chunk of boards together, the rising chatter of attempted intimidation. Fifty surfers paddled toward shore. The wave crept in, rose under them, lifted them—amazingly—a foot in the air. Poor, back-broken wave!

FANTASEA

There was light ahead, a distinct spot of it in the blackness, growing larger. Timothy plodded on, sloshing through warm water, his heart beating faster.

The light grew to a circle. The circle grew to a vista: the rust-colored liquid of the Continental Gap. What was once called Ocean.

He stood in the mouth of the huge stainless-steel pipe, then threw out his board and dove after it.

Entry was warm and slimy. He exhaled immediately to avoid ingestion, then surfaced and swept the shit from the ribbed deck of his board, combed it with his fingers from his hair. He scrambled up onto the board, sat up and looked out toward the end of the breakwall where three-foot waves crumbled over in perfect form, bursting into luminous orange foam.

Beautiful! he thought. And no one else out there!

He wondered if Joan was watching, turned and scanned the shoreline. At water's edge, in both directions as far as the eye could see, were hundred-story apartment dwellings, a great wall of windows. He tried to locate his, despaired, then turned and paddled toward the end of the breakwall, muttering in his mind the great words of Surf-Father John Severson:

"In this crowded world the surfer can still seek and find the perfect day, the perfect wave, and be alone with the surf and his thoughts . . . "

SPACE

The eye moves towards a Galaxy.

The Galaxy swirls like a cyclone of electric dust, swiftly in the blackness. It awaits you like a grinding whirlpool, huge amidst an infinite void. Huge enough to suck an eye into existence. Huge enough and strong enough to wrench you from Eternity, Infinitely even, and suck you into living. Into shape. Into reality. Down.

DREAM

We pray, our bodies together in love, and then we go to the water to ride the waves. Warm water rings our legs, rising as we enter. The offshore wind gently buffets our skin, teases our hair, encourages our passions.

We paddle through the channel and out along the point. All the way to the lineup we are looking sideways into the eyes of perfect waves. There is the clean smell of foam, salty and warm. We are together in our happiness.

SHARED DREAM

Wading into the piddling shorebreak, there was no room to paddle out. When I finally caught a wave, the guy in front of me was a total kook, just waiting for the plunging lip to knock his board out from under him, and the guy behind me was some hotshot asshole from the Valley who kept roller-coastering down onto the tail of my board. To complicate matters, my leg was tangled up in my surf leash.

FANTASEA

Larry waited in line, his teeth clenched tight, his gut knotted. It was ten minutes until Surf Hour ended and the Grem was hassling over some kid's license.

There was the huge boom of the wave generator and a hiss as a new swell was born. Ten riders surfed it, shooting back and forth and around each other.

Finally, Grem let the kid pass; the line inched forward. The Grem checked ten more IDs, then stopped the line by pulling a red, white, and blue cord across the entrance. Those waiting fidgeted. Those inside took positions in the water and switched on their power cells. When the first wave passed into the Safe Zone, a buzzer echoed in the Dome, and the generator birthed another wave.

Ten more surfers were admitted. Larry waited, third in the next group. The buzzer sounded; the plunger went WOMB!

"Okay . . . Okay . . . Hold it," the Grem said, placed an open hand on Larry's chest. "That's not a conventional." He pointed at Larry's board. "Sorry, no entry."

"But . . ."

His fingers pressed into Larry's chest, pushing him back, out of the way of others. "Sorry!" he insisted.

Larry resisted. "I'll ride over on the other side, out of the . . ."

"Conventionals only!" the Grem snapped. "Must have power cell. Cannot make exception. Sorry!" He jabbed his fingertips hard into Larry's chest, so that Larry staggered backwards and turned with tears in his eyes and five white spots on his enraged red chest.

SPACE

Were you hypnotized by the Azure Pearl? How came you here?

You are your eye, now in the Air of the Earth, flying over Water. You are

Fire, consuming what you see.

You are flying swiftly; your hair blows behind you like flames. A breeze from a distant hurricane . . . an echo of the speed of light growing closer. The hair in your eye blows.

DREAM

We are giddy in our stomachs as we approach the lineup, slide up the face of a perfect wave, and look in! An eight-foot-wide hole in the water, a nebula of foam living in the pit of it. And beyond it, another one outside! And another beyond . . . and another!

SHARED DREAM

The son-of-a-bitch hit me! I felt my nose go all crunchy and my head was about to explode.

I reached down into the water and grabbed a big, gnarly rock. First it wouldn't give, but then it came out of its socket like a stone eye, and I brought it out and up by my ear and looked at him.

He was scared now that he saw the rock.

I touched my left hand under my nose, and it came away all covered with blood. The blood looked sort of watery. It dribbled down my fingers and off into the water. I thought about all the ways I could smash his face—bashed in and ripped apart, the possible uses of my surf leash—his face swollen red and eyes bugged out. And then I flashed . . . in my mind I had pictured doing all this to him, but it wasn't him. It wasn't his face, it was mine!

FANTASEA

There were many reasons why Craig jumped ship, most of them implanted in his head when he was young, reading Joseph Conrad and Jack London.

But even his fantaseas were not up to the splendor of the reality. Floundering desperately in the aerated turmoil of the ship's wake, he clawed to the fizzing surface to see the supertanker growing smaller, its deep whining sound fading into the distance.

He turned and located the spot of land he would try for.

He was detached enough to enjoy what he was doing. It would be valuable experience, if he made it.

He stripped off his clothes and began to swim, smiling at the happy thought that there were no longer any sharks to worry about. In London's time, he would have been eaten before he bobbed to the surface. Now there was just the swim to worry about. He was happy that he was not panicking. That made it all the easier.

He swam for hours. Saw the low smudge of land grow into a humped form. Saw the yellowy foam bursting away at its beaches. Saw the even sweep of shit-brown sand. He smiled and swam and at sundim crawled ashore. He pulled himself as far up the slime-slick beach as possible, then lost consciousness.

In the morning he was bitten awake by the flies. In the opaque light of day he saw that he was on land, a large island of dirt and rock devoid of any vegetation. No animal, no bird, no insects save the flies.

But still, better than life in one of the buttresses. Better by far than that, he smiled. It had been a long time since he had seen anything living besides Human Resource Units. These flies would be a comfort to him—sensation while he watched the rusty waves. The only man in the Continental Gap . . . an adventure beyond London's dreams! Dying alone!

SPACE

Soar above the ragged line where Land and Water meet. Glide along a long, long way, eye of mind following the shape of a world, planet third from Sol, perfect azure pearl fluffed with swirling white vapors. Fly above this miracle in a void, this Eden-perfect gift where life is graced with ultimate potential, where mind is free to rise from matter, to manifest itself as God or Source or simple Being. Beyond language and idea.

DREAM

We ride in the eye, feeling joy beyond laughter. Knowing we are as close to our Godselves as we can be without another of us. The perfect moment goes on and on. A mile of perfect moments, under folding liquid glass, in the sun. Riding like the current in a wire. Flying like a message to ourselves. Finding a new and ancient reality at the limits of imagination.

SHARED DREAM

I forgave; I forgot. I dropped the rock. So what? I pushed my nose into its rightful shape and left the water. I hopped from red light to red light to the hospital. I went to Emergency and showed my nose.

A doctor asked how it happened.

"I did it surfing," I said.

He asked about my insurance: "Does it cover Acts of God?"

FANTASEA

Tired of studying, tired of bullshit, Stan slapped off his text tape and stripped away his clothes. I need a surf, he thought. I really need a surf. He left the room in his robe.

Things had become so oppressive in his life; in everyone's life. There seemed to be no texture to existence anymore. No variety, no surprises, no adventure. Year after year, most of it Private Time, and nothing to do with it.

Except surf.

He took the elevator down eighty-seven flights, got out, and walked down the long hallway. It was worth it, he thought. A lot of guys on his floor never got into surfing because of the walk. They were more into the Power Games, like anyone else. Power Games on every floor, he thought. Rooms with bright red doors.

He opened the green door marked "Surfing."

A few friends turned and nodded, smiling broadly, obviously stoked.

He slid in next to Kenny.

"How's it?" he asked.

Kenny disconnected and said, "What?"

"How is it?"

"Six foot tubes. Ranch Reef Selects," he answered, then hooked up again, saying, "C'mon, there's a set!"

Stan hung his robe on the hook, put his hands and feet into the receivers, and lay back naked into the Sensory Bubble. His head dropped back, releasing the probes that sprung from the headrest and bristled against his scalp. He hooked up just in time to ride a perfect wave with the others. A very close relationship, he thought happily—sharing a tube with friends.

Each surfer lay back in his own Sensory Bubble, transported into the same place on the same wave. Each being the rider, and therefore being each other. It was a very full experience and they had grown close over the years, even though few were locals on this floor and the others were scattered throughout the Megaminium.

After the session everyone talked about the waves, describing ledges and sections and tubes that had been made. Everyone had hit bottom on one eight-footer.

Everyone swam after the board that had washed up on the sand in front of the woman they all knew was Circe. Everyone sat to talk, heard her offer, accepted it, and made love to her.

Then everyone paddled out again.

Back in his apartment, later, Stan felt penned in and claustrophobic. As much as he enjoyed surfing, it nearly always made him feel this way—anxious and tense, as if there were something he was missing. Something he should be doing but wasn't. Some lack of fullness after all.

He rode the lift to the roof, went out into the heavy air, and milled about with the others. He saw no one he knew in the dusky dimness. The roof lights were blobs of yellowish red dullness, and today he could not see across the Airway to the opposite Megaminium. The traffic itself was a dim motion. It was not the clearest day of the year, that was for sure.

Then there was a piercing wail and immediately the crowd started milling toward the exits. The Noon Whistle. Time for lunch.

This story originally appeared in the December/January issue of Surfing *magazine 1972–73 and has been revised.*

the kook

SCUM-EYED, BLUE IN THE FACE, fingertips dancing on a frosty garbage can lid, Casey stood and watched blue puffs of mist pull back from cracking curls as his own breath pumped clouds into the immediate foreground, misting his thick glasses. From one end to the other, the broad sands of Main Beach were as empty as Casey's pockets, which were every bit as empty as his stomach.

He tucked his mouth down behind the sweatshirt zipper and breathed the ice that clumped there, melting it to water. He pulled the hood low over his forehead and looked around, back up over the town to where the ridgeline of the hills was as clean and sharp as the morning air. The sun was about to rise. Or, as the narrator in his brain stated: "The rotation of the planetary ball upon which you are now standing is bringing you back into the direct radiation of the nearest star, thus bringing to an end 14 hours and 23 minutes of night." The days are short in January.

His beat, old pickup stood alone in the parking lot; it had been there since yesterday afternoon. He'd surfed till dark and returned to find the battery utterly dead. It was a cold night, in the mid-20s, but there was no snow and very little ice. The local atmosphere was dominated by a large high-pressure system. Humidity was in the teens—no precipitation in almost a month, and straight-offshore winds every morning with not a cloud in the sky.

He had been teaching himself to surf since summer ended and the beach drained itself of people. The local pack had stayed around to enjoy the crisp autumn waves, until around Thanksgiving; they all disappeared about the time the water chilled to 40. He saw a few of them once in a while, but no one ever paddled out now. Or, as the narrator stated: "The experiential downside of the surfing experience in this place and time has exceeded all cumulative motivational factors resulting in a counter-inertial moment indicating stasis pending significant reversals of said factors (or the emergence of a new factor or factors) historically associated with the fourth month and the Vernal Equinox." In short, the place was his.

"Oh, for a decent wetsuit!" his frosted balls cried out. "Oh, for a strong battery—a Die-Hard perchance—to crank the starter to fire the engine to boil the antifreeze to warm the car's heater and thereby thaw my stiffening flesh!" his numbed toes intoned. Forget about what his mouth tried to say—the fountains were frozen, all faucets welded by the season. There was nothing to do about any of it. "You may as well go surfing," said the narrator in his brain.

There was another problem: his wetsuit was as solid as a board. If he tried to put it on, arms and legs would break off like icicles from rain gutters. As for his board—all orange twin-fin Fish, ancient relic of a mysto Cliff-dwelling era, passed backwards down the hierarchy until it came at last into his hands for 20 garage-sale dollars on a warm summer's afternoon—the deck was a crystallized sheet of frozen wax, slick as a rink. "Hmmm," spoke the narrator. "Each moment is an equation. You'll figure it out."

He yanked the door open and undressed, standing on his old shoes while his blue eyes patrolled the parking lot. He left on his briefs, grabbed the stiff towel from the seat, and bent it around his waist. It curled as if it were sculpted to look windblown. He worked his numb feet into the shoes, then put his glasses on the dash and slammed the door. He went around to pull his board and wetsuit out of the back. The offshore wind burned his naked skin, so the board's icy kiss against his ribs was hardly remarkable. He held the wetsuit and boots away from his body with the other hand while he scampered through the gap in the wall and down to the churning water.

The beach was still deserted as he dropped the surfboard and towel on the frozen sand and hobbled into the ocean on numb feet. He flipped the boots just out of reach of the waves as the first surge of whitewater wrapped around his ankles like a balm. Compared to the sand and the air, it was bath water. He dunked the wetsuit into the water and massaged it back into rubber, then pulled it on as he stood there trying to maintain his balance in the ebb and flow. It was a struggle.

He pulled the hood over his head—his hair felt as brittle as he did—and gathered up the boots. He took a glove out of each, sloshed them all back to life, then sat on the hard sand and put them on—boots, then gloves.

That felt better, although the narrator cautioned: "The ratio of calories expended in maintaining survivable core temp to intake of fuel suggests an imminent energy shortage. Try kelp." A few small green bulbs and dark, crimped leaves, silvered with frost, were scattered at the tide line, so he picked them up, flicked off the sand, and ate them—cold on his teeth like frozen grapes, but they were good, and the salt seemed to soothe something in him.

He flopped the surfboard upside-down onto a surge, held it there for a while, then brought it back to the beach to try to rub some texture into it with a handful of sand. It was like trying to rub scratches in glass, and he gave up rather quickly since his arms immediately tired.

He took another look up and down the beach and up towards his car (he could just see the roof of the cab over the seawall) and the town, with the sun lifting over the ridge—blinding him with its welcome promise of warmth. He could feel it press against his black-suited chest, forcing out an involuntary sigh of pleasure, a little "Mmmm." And then he plunged back into the ocean with intent. He knew what to do. He had it wired.

Driving from the garage sale to the beach on that hot July afternoon, the Fish loosely cradled in back, echoing every bump in the road with a thump of its own, he was in a thrill of anticipation, dying to cool off and "walk on water." But Main Beach was a zoo, it took almost an hour to park and get down to the water, and then he met the locals.

"Asshole!" was the first thing he heard as he pushed his board through the shorebreak, walking it across the sandbar towards deeper water. He looked left to see a kid in baggy trunks and a white rash-guard ricocheting off a small chunk of whitewater. About two minutes later, another kid, coming from the opposite side, didn't say a word as he fell backward off his tiny thruster and sent its sharpened beak twirling towards Casey's head.

It was the same all up and down the beach—unless the black ball was flying, and then the circus moved to the parking lot where everything about him—from his cut-off Levi's trunks to his orange Fish—seemed worthy of ridicule. After a couple of months of this, he came to accept that the only way he was ever going to learn to surf was to wait for winter.

But it didn't take that long. Before September was over, he found peaks to himself, and he practiced paddling, catching waves—proning, then standing. By November he could sort of surf; by Thanksgiving he was alone.

Now he was out of work and out of money, and he didn't know what to do.

The only place he had to call his own—outside of the front seat of his truck—was the arching face of an incoming wave. As the narrator in his brain stated: "The ephemeral nature of these substantially imaginative encounters with waves approaches the illusory, yet the real-time neural stimulation and restorative prophylaxis suggests concrete uploading of significant bioremedial components, resulting in a stunning net profit on time and energy invested."

When the lull came, he paddled neatly out between the little peaks and put himself in position for the next five-foot set. He was lining up his car with the phone pole next to the liquor store when he noticed the other car pull into the lot; there were boards on top.

They sat in the car—Chewy, Louie, and Dewey—listening to Rage Against The Machine's "Bulls on Parade," heater cranking on high, chowing down on jelly donuts and coffee.

"Clean!" said Louie.

"One guy out," said Chewy.

"Freezin'," said Dewey.

"He's goin'!" said Chewy.

They watched through the windshield as Casey windmilled awkwardly into the wave and pushed down the face. They saw how he struggled stiffly to his feet and angled to the left, how he got briefly slotted, tried to straighten off, was nailed by the lip, and crashed.

"What a kook!" said Dewey. He put the car in gear and headed out of the lot.

This story first appeared in the March 2000 issue of Surfer *magazine.*

the life and times
of a last-ditch yogi

HIS SPIRITUAL AND CORPOREAL ASSETS have been compounded quarterly since the beginning. The interest alone now fills six Swiss banks and a coterie of massage parlor vestibules in the City of Angels. He speaks always in a single tongue.

"I started surfing in 1958," the Yogi recently replied in an interview with *Time* magazine, who kept fanning his pages back and forth between People, Sports, Religion, and Modern Living, not sure, really, where a surfing yogi actually belonged.

"Gads!" cried the Yogi in a misty-eyed revelry, spacing out on those good ol' days. "It was just—just—er—great! I hit a ninth-level samadhi just waxing my board!"

At the time of the interview, the Yogi was refueling his Lamborghini at a Terrible Herbst self-service gas station on La Brea Boulevard. The smog was so thick you would have needed a machete to cut the air. Gas was pouring out of the side of the car all over the Yogi's feet, but he didn't seem to notice, perhaps because his long gray beard was blowing all over his face.

Back on the Santa Monica Freeway, the Yogi wove a neatly intricate path through rush-hour traffic down to the Pacific Coast Highway. The smell of gas in the car was incredible, but the Yogi kept smiling. With the windows down, *Time* magazine fluttered and snapped as the brisk breeze riffled through The Nation to The World.

"300 billion sold!" marveled the Yogi.

"300 billion what?" queried *Time* magazine in a concerted effort at journalistic self-control, despite a rip in Cinema.

"McDonald's!" explained the yet marveling Yogi. "I suppose . . . well . . . ah . . . er . . . I dunno . . . I suppose hamburgers . . . or Big Macs . . . or . . . or all together, I suppose."

Down the beach, just past Synanon House near the Bel-Aire Beach Club, they got down to the issues.

"I don't think surfers should get money for surfing until they're over thirty," the Yogi said to *Time* magazine. "I think that surfing magazines are a cheap shot and shouldn't run advertisements or articles. I think Australia is a good place for Santa Monica surfers to move. I think the owners of Ranch property should throw an annual picnic for all the surfers of the world! I think that surfers should not, repeat should not, repeat repeat should not evacuate their snot in the lineup. I think that older gentlemen with beards should have the right-of-way regardless. I think that Mickey Dora, who is a hoax and who never really existed (as he himself well knows), should go left for the rest of his earthly sentence. I don't think surfers should require sex or cigarettes. I think the Coast Highway should be given back to the Chumash Indians and Los Angeles turned back into a tar pit. I think the Valley is where it's happening and everyone should retire there. I think cars are still too cheap and gas is still too expensive—what's that smell? I think waves should be declared an endangered species and fenced off to protect them. What else?"

Time magazine thought for a minute, then asked: "But what about the Dream that we all had?"

"To prefer this dream to that dream is of no consequence. That's exactly why I can drive a Lamborghini and throw my hamburger wrappers out the window."

"But that's littering," gasped *Time* magazine.

"Ah, yes," sighed the Yogi, "but Rome is falling."

This story originally appeared in H_2O *magazine in 1976.*

a wave in search of the perfect surfer
(a message from the medium)

I WAS SPAWNED IN THE NORTH PACIFIC Ocean in early December. My mother the ocean, my father a fierce, relentless (27.96 inches of mercury by the barometer) Low Pressure. In fact, my parents had one of the stormiest relationships ever recorded in the history of wind and sea.

I was blasted out of the womb by a 240-mile-per-hour gust that sent me overtaking other sibling waves. Father kept huffing and puffing at me for miles and miles, as if to say "good riddance, be gone," but I know better now. He infused me with his strength, and by the time I pulled out from under his shadow I was a solid 40-foot swell, a band of energy radiating from its source that any parent would have been proud of.

In those first few hours and days I passed soundlessly through bottomless waters. In one sense I was free of my mother; in a larger sense I was still rooted in her and, indeed, my body was her body. As for my father, he had given me direction and force, and his power was, to a certain extent, held within me like a massive charge of dynamite.

The vessels that I encountered, like tiny leaves scattered on the sea, ran with me, heading south. I found the sensation of lifting them and carrying them forward to be exhilarating, as if I could experience my own movement through them.

It was a shock, however, to discover that some of these vessels were simply overwhelmed by me. "The boy doesn't know his own strength" is a phrase that comes to mind, and yet there was nothing that could be done; I was what I was as I am what I am, and if ships and sailors were sent forever into the belly of my mother, then that was the price that was exacted from all concerned, and what could be done about it? I know, too, that in my early hours, in the frenzy of birth, in the swirl of the spiral nest, it was precarious for all concerned. Billions of infinitesimal wave-possibilities came into being, then were swallowed by other wave-possibilities, and then those wave-possibilities were swallowed by still others.

Certainly there was no choice in the matter.

And yet, I must admit, that at a certain stage, when I began to feel myself as a wave with its own direction, identity, and possibilities, I began also to experience a certain remorse for those smaller waves (some scarcely ripples) that I was forced and propelled to overtake and consume. And yet they too became a part of what I was (what I am). Their energy eventually became mine. And how can I even say "mine"? After all, what I call "mine" is simply the sum of all these other waves that make me up. What I call "I" is simply all these little waves.

So sometimes I wished to go no further, to eat no more of these little waves, to engulf no more ships. Or, at other times, I wished to be gobbled by another, larger, following wave. But it never came, and I continued on.

Vast and unresisting was the medium through which I moved; of it and in it both at the same time. Far from my whirling source, each hour brought greater definition, greater solidarity to my mass. I sensed the bands of welted sea that ran before me and behind me (my brothers and sisters), and our mass and strength transformed the calm sea into alternating peak and trough with no flat surface in between. Indeed, we were our father's children.

I suppose that it would be quite impossible to describe in words what I have come to see as my first great experience, and how it drew me with astonishment and, for the first time, gave me the rare glimpse of what I truly was.

It was as if something had entered me, punctured me in some way. My broad, unfocused vision suddenly was coalesced, gathered, at one single point in my expanding, stretching anatomy. Naturally, I felt that I was wounded, had stumbled in some way, and might be left behind. The bottomless ocean was bottomless no longer; there was a definite limit, and I touched it. How can I describe the emotions? It was, at first, like a convulsion: an anxiety that built and grew taut and, then, gave. I opened in a flood of relief and something in me sensed (how, I do not know) that this was Land, and that Land meant my Death, and at the same time represented my possibilities.

I am just a wave, and none of this comes easily to me, yet the incredible sweetness and familiarity of that first touch of land thrilled me with its implications. I gave into the sensation; there was nothing else that I could do. My whole awareness went into that part of me that had touched Land, to that part of me that lifted itself out of the rest of me and heaved out a portion of the Father that was stored in the whole of me.

I felt my entire body wrap around this penetrating point of Land; I wrapped along its reefs and shores. Oh, I was sure that I was slain, that it had killed me. So you can imagine my amazement when the touch of Land passed away and my body was miraculously joined again into one, the two open sides merging together, leaving no trace. It was an Island! Exquisite!

I must admit I had been frightened, terrified in fact. Now there was a giddy joy. Islands! Experiences! Things that would involve me, test my strength, give me expression, and from which I might recover and continue, having survived it all. And to know that the other waves must pass around these same Islands! Crash against those same reefs and cliffs; sigh upon, caress, and lunge upon those same soft beaches! How much more was this than just an open sea! I felt that I had found the meaning of existence and surged inevitably onwards, open to whatever Fate would place in my path, and beginning to realize that other waves were already living what I would live tomorrow.

My revelry was interrupted by a tugging, a bending at the shoulders. A huge, long part of me began to slow and drag, stretching me thinner and thinner at the extremities while the central thrust of me bore on. And then so soon thereafter my other shoulder sagged with the weight of bottom, of Land, drawing thin that other part of me as well. How interesting to notice in the flutters of panic how my attention shifted, first to one vast shoulder, then to another, then to the inexorable center somehow bearing on to the South, so utterly unaffected. I was as a gull, who first in even flight soars squarely in the wind, then seeing something below, banks over into a dive with wings swept back and beak extended towards the mark. Such were the sensations as my right shoulder sounded upon Asia and my left upon North America, while my center sought new Islands, relentlessly, to the South.

This pulling at the shoulders was a different kind of thing than my first encounter with an Island. Something here was much more final, more absolute. Here were definite limits, channeling me for the first time. It was Land, and so, in a way, it was Death and yet it was a different kind of Death. More like the Death of certain possibilities, which seemed to confine and direct me at the same time, and even to strengthen my Southern force.

It was, in fact, along my left shoulder, as I wound along the Canadian, and then the Californian coasts, that my attention detected a previously undetected energy and presence, which provided a meaning for those incredible moments where I was opened to (what else can I call it?) higher possibilities.

At first it felt as some intrusion, if salt perhaps was sprinkled in a wound. Something touching just that part of me that sensed most deeply that expression of emotion associated with my father (for, clearly, these places of eruption, of touching reef and land, were nothing if not emotions), filling me with a haunting music, as if my body had become an instrument for some alien musician. And yet he played me well, this alien musician, and he strangely chose to play me in a place where the shape of Land and bottom had evoked from me precisely my highest and my best. In some way he was in that delicate space between my flesh and blood, between my thoughts and emotions, between my body and my soul.

You see, before this, as when the Island opened me to myself, I thought that that was the whole of it, that the sensations of division and of union were an end in themselves. And now for the first time I learned that these experiences, these openings, were provided so that something higher and finer could enter in to that place of my deepest vulnerability.

And, too, I found that if I put the whole of my attention upon that fine energy that had entered there, I could perceive more clearly what the essence of it was. And the answer came that it was many things, different at different times, yet it was always a Rider of Waves.

The first to ride me was a black-suited solitary rider, where I wrapped around Vancouver Island, raising the icy waters as I passed through. The rider stayed somewhat out of the vortex of my open end, yet close enough to taste some of what I had brought from the North Pacific. Yet, as I said before, he touched the quick of me on occasion and made me aware of the space between flesh and blood, thought and emotion, body and soul.

And, of course, you would not think that a wave had these separate parts; you would think, perhaps, that only humans had them. But I bear you the tidings that all things have them, and a wave no differently, though different words describe identical phenomena, on different scales. So my flesh is water, my blood is my movement; my thought is my shape, my emotion my eruption; my body is my mother, my soul is my father. Much like you, perhaps.

The drag of Continental Shelf held my shoulder back ever further as I swept by Oregon, in and out of cove, around point, along straight white beach, and here and there now was the penetrating entry of the Riders of the Waves. All in rubber, black and shivering and exhilarated they rode me, their movements somewhat angular and strained in the cold water, and my mass was no threat by this time, as I had stretched out so far I was scarcely an 8-foot wave when I peeled by the Golden Gate.

How strange it was then to feel this same occurrence, the entry of a surfer into my emotional space, at the extreme other end of my body, where unwound a 10-foot spiral off Japan. Like a mirror to my other half there first appeared the sensation, then the feeling of this penetration. My attention was immediately thrown into conflict and was pulled back and forth between the two experiences, creating quite an unusual psychological state in me, as if I were being pulled apart in yet another way. Just at that moment my Southern-most center touched reef off the Hawai'ian Islands and my attention was pulled back into that part of me.

What to do? How many places could I be at once? Everything felt so amazingly complicated, and then suddenly, something in me broke. My attention blossomed out from the center in both directions, and I was, for the first time that I could remember, aware of the whole expanse of my necklace-like body at the same time. At the same instant that I was being ridden in Japan and ridden in California, a surfer found an open, curling part of me at Hanalei Bay on Kauai, where my mass was still quite concentrated and I stood up at nearly twenty-five feet. The feeling of being touched in such a powerful place was overwhelming and, yes, exquisite too, and yet at the peripheries of me the two riders, in Japan and California, presented a subtle depth that increased my total sense of presence all the more. Never had I been so aware of myself. So I stormed around Kauai while peeling off both distant continents, now being ridden in a dozen places by at least twenty-four riders.

And then I was tantalized by a most delicious thought, an incredible realization: that these surfers knew nothing of one another. That each supposed he rode this wave alone, had me to himself. (I must admit that here I giggled at the thought and blasted three surfers over the falls at Steamer Lane in Santa Cruz. Passing by I heard one call out in anger, blaming his wipeout on the kelp!)

I remembered then an earlier realization: that I was made up of all the many little waves that I had overtaken and assimilated, and this new situation felt similar. I now felt that I was somehow composed of all the surfers who were riding me at a given moment, maybe of all the surfers who would ride me in the space between the stormy womb and the last reef that I would break upon. And, too, I was aware that I was so many different things in different places.

Peeling off near Santa Barbara, I was a perfect point wave, with a complicated network of interlacing tracks working the thundering heart of me. And then I was a giddy, peaky beachbreak in South East Asia, where my size surprised and challenged a lone surfer (I tried to use my will for him and hold myself so perfectly open; I think I did well; I think he appreciated), and peak and channel, peak and channel gave me a delicate sense of myself. And then I touched reef off the North Shore of Oahu and was surprised to learn something so new in myself: something larger and stronger than I had imagined rose up out of me, raged over and battered itself mercilessly onto the coral. It seemed almost bizarre and surreal that even here, at Sunset and Waimea and Banzai, surfers committed themselves into the wrathful, vicious core of me, and taunted me (what else might I call it?) with their presence in the very whirlpool of my life. Only off Kaena Point was my display unridden, and there my violence grew to such a state that later I was embarrassed at the memory. So when I rounded into Makaha I made myself rideable again and was relieved to feel the current of fine energy working again the face of my uplifted body.

But then, far off on my right, a series of terrible amputations occurred, as Islands intertwined with other Islands and broke off parts of me that were never to return to other parts. For awhile my awareness went with them, but as they spilled their last in empty coves, in dark, murky bays, I left them to themselves. Though still the memory is strong of one quite unexpected rider, off in one maze-tangled corner of the Pacific, who rode me like no other had, in long, stinging-quick strides, deeper than ever before, yet beyond capture, far, far from anyone's awareness but his own and scarcely noticed by me at first, but charming me soon with his dexterity. The feeling came that somehow this surfer had made sense out of me in ways that I could not have made sense out of myself. And as that part of me died in that cove, and as that rider completed his ride, something in me felt tinged with incompleteness, and my "eye" sought out for another such rider to duplicate that experience, to make sense of my purpose. For I could no longer make sense of it myself.

So it was that I came to realize that experiences (touching reef, lifting, heaving, exploding) were not in themselves enough. They did not explain me; there was something else. And these surfers were a part of that, these Riders of Waves. For insignificant as they were alone, together, working a wave simultaneously, they were a communications device that transmitted the energy of my father to the Land in a way that my spilling up onto the beach could never accomplish.

Too bad that I realized this past my prime, past Hawai'i. Though since, I have seen that this was the only way it could have been. Each awareness must come in its turn, each experience admits the material for understanding the next experience. Or, rather, it can if we allow that material to enter. But I was just a wave. Heaven knows, there have been many since me as there were many before. And though I was a fine wave, and a strong, powerful one, that had nothing to do with any choice of mine. I was simply propelled through the marvelous medium of the sea.

I think it was somewhere off Fiji, maybe nearing Australia, that I first understood where I had made a basic mistake. You see, back in the Islands I had assumed that when I grew monstrous and violent on the North Shore, and eventually unrideable at Kaena, I had a choice in the matter. But later I made the inevitable connection: the reef was there waiting, so was the Island. My mass was predetermined by the abruptness of the change of depths, the presence or absence of Islands in my path, the continuity of my length. When this predetermined mass touched the waiting obstacle, the result was inevitable. It is difficult to say how much this realization at first tormented me, or how much it later relieved me. Suffice to say that at first I found this realization quite upsetting because for so long that part of me that I call "attention," or "mind," had taken credit for these outbursts. I had taken credit for my size, shape, power, even for my direction. So this was hard to let go of.

Yet, when I began to let go of this illusion, something much more real took its place: I saw what I could control and what I could not control. And what I could control, all that I could control, was my awareness of all that occurred to me and awareness of myself passing through these many unavoidable and predetermined experiences. Much like you perhaps? It struck me that I was not the wave, and I was not the surfer, and I was not the reefs and islands and coves. I was nothing that I could put my finger on, to use a phrase, but was, quite simply one "eye" in an ocean of "eyes." And sometimes this eye saw more, sometimes less. That much seemed up to me. Whoever "me" was, or is.

I could try to describe to you, you who may be a Rider of Waves, the peace of those last hours of my life, heading into the thickening chill waters of the Antarctic and the clear white light of eventual nothingness. But it would be impossible.

I could mention that I went without resignation, yet with acceptance. Seeing what I was not helped me to see what I was. And I was the whole ocean, and I was none of it.

I could also say that the Riders of Waves are the messengers of the sea. They create a higher possibility for a wave. Just as a wave creates a higher possibility for a Rider of Waves. But that sounds like another paradox. So we will step around it.

And so, in my final dissipation, I came to realize that what would continue of me was what would be remembered by those who had ridden me.

Like all waves, I was the sum of the rides I had given—the moments of memory that would exist in the minds of surfers and those who watched as I rolled by. For the rest of it, perhaps I did not exist at all.

This story first appeared in the December/January issue of Surfing *magazine,* 1976–77.

the mythology of surfing

So Zeus wedded Hera. Out of this connection two sons were born at one birth—Dylan and Lleu, who are considered as representing the twin powers of darkness and light. With darkness the sea was inseparably connected by the Celts, and as soon as the dark twin was born and named, he plunged headlong into his native element. "And immediately when he was in the sea," says the Mabinogi of Mâth, son of Mâthonwy, "he took its nature, and swam as well as the best fish that was therein. And for that reason was he called Dylan, the Son of the Wave. Beneath him no wave ever broke." He was killed with a spear at last by his uncle, Govannan, and, according to the bard Taliesin, the waves of Britain, Ireland, Scotland, and the Isle of Man wept for him.*

Beautiful legends grew up around his death. The clamor of the waves dashing upon the beach is the expression of their longing to avenge their son. The sound of the sea rushing up the mouth of the River Conway is still known as "Dylan's Death-Groan."**

*Book of Taliesin, XLIII, "The Death Song of Dylan, Son of the Wave," from *The Four Ancient Books of Wales.*

**Prof. John Rhys, "The Hibbert Lectures," Oxford University Press, 1886.

STRANGE THAT IN EACH SMALL MOMENT of our lives, aware of it or not, we are the actors in some primal, archetypal play. Strange that all the fundamental relationships articulated in the classical mythologies—Vedic, Greek, Roman, Norse, Chinese, and others—are acted out again and again in our daily lives, on the scale of our personal fates. On any given day we may well experience the same mythic principles and forces encountered by Hercules, Perseus, Pandora, and the others, without realizing it. We are blinded, merely, by the difference in scale—the superhuman deeds of those ancients versus the rather mundane actions of our ordinary lives.

But, as Hermes Trismegistus once said, "As above, so below." So it is that even ordinary lives are infused with the same laws that govern the mythic and the epic. It's worlds within worlds, and the play remains the same. There are only so many combinations of possibilities, and these recur again and again through time, on a variety of different scales, and because the scales are different, we fail to recognize the essential unity of the underlying laws and principles and see only the differences in scale and manifestation.

The lesson of mythology may be, in part, to reconnect what has been scattered. To gather the random notes into a total harmony, chord, or refrain. To demonstrate that the mythological essence held within all beings determines the dimensions of possible action.

It may not be surprising to discover that surfing does, indeed, possess a very real mythology. At first this seems quite apparent: the ancient Hawai'ian myths of Naihe, Moikeha, Kelea, and Maui, of Kahekilani and Bird Maiden, who turned one surfer to stone at Sunset Beach. But there are possibly even greater myths, like the Celtic legend referenced earlier. These are myths more ancient than the Hawai'ians, more obscure than the Greek, Roman, or Vedic, and more fundamental than one might realize.

In ancient times, before recorded history, men apparently possessed the quite practical knowledge (rediscovered by Albert Einstein in the early 1900s) that the universe is composed of waves, that waves manifest in spirals, and that all things recur again and again because of this. In fact, the most enlightened humans have always understood the role of waves and cycles in determining the law of all action throughout the universe. Wave, vibration, undulation: the movement of the sea.[1]

Waves manifest in all the large and small things of our lives. Hours, days, weeks, months, years; feast and famine; war and peace; birth and death; storm and clear: all is waves. Waves in your coffee cup, waves in your thoughts, waves in your days in the world. Waves to wake you, waves to shake you, waves to rock you, waves to take you.

⁂

The rider of waves is descended from the one twin of Zeus, the Lord of the Gods: Dylan, the Child of Darkness, the Son of the Wave. Born in the ether, the vapor, the buffeting wind, free from fault he entered the sea to balance the Child of Light. He entered the sea and in so doing, he entered another world, and waves were as much a part of the new world as the other, and he rode them, as all humans ride them—in the biggest cities, on the flattest flatlands, and upon the highest mountains (every night and day a wave, every thought, every taste, every feeling a wave) where it all rolled by below and above.

Dylan was "never known to make a foolish move," so why did his uncle Govannan (Jokerman?) slay him? Why a spear? As any surfer knows, a spear is a very narrow, pointed surfboard. It is a most curious tale.

⁂

Poseidon, the Lord of the Sea, is mythically remembered for driving over the oceans in his golden chariot, quelling the thunder of the waves as he went, collapsing waves into stillness with a thrust of his trident. Other times he created storms as he went, conjuring the water up out of itself, heaping it into thundering mounds of swell and surf. (It is said it was he also who gave man the first horse.) Poseidon was the brother of Zeus and thereby also Dylan's uncle.

Dylan was surfing a long time before man (as he is today) appeared on the earth. Weary of surfing alone, he sought fellowship with men and provided them with vessels to ride upon the waves. Poseidon, a jealous god who had given man horses precisely to keep him out of the sea, hurled one of these first vessels (the "spear") at Dylan and killed him. Poseidon preferred Dylan's brother, Lleu, the Child of Light, who kept out of his way.

It was an Infinite Moment: Dylan was surfing off the coast of France, somewhat out of his usual territory. He had already taught humans to surf in Ireland, Scotland, England, and the Isle of Man (though in those times the whole area was referred to as L'Etolle, "the school"), and now he wished to teach in France. Geographically, things were different then; there was no Iberian Peninsula, no Portugal or Spain. Rather, Etolle was much larger than it is today, and the ocean around it was called Bombora.

Dylan had found a student and had begun to teach. They were in the water for some time before the learner could master the vessel at all, for Dylan could only show a person, he could not do it for him. Finally, they were up and riding, streaking along a solid 10-foot wall, Dylan working in and out of the back of the wave, doing reverse floaters and cutback loops and generally ripping (with the student trying just to stay on a track, succeeding with occasional nudges from the teacher, who was both in and out of the wave).

Towards the end of the ride, where the wave went hollow and sucked out over the reef, barreling faster and faster, Poseidon slipped onto the scene and touched the tail of the student's surfboard with his trident, exploding it out from under him and into the back of Dylan, who was dissolved from this plane to recur in a slightly higher role: as a late-twentieth-century poet from the Northern Woods named Zimmerman.

However, Dylan's students had the taste of it—surfing—and they continued to ride waves after the master's departure. And these students attracted others who began to ride the waves as Dylan had taught them. But after a time, a dangerous situation arose—Poseidon became aware of disturbances in the Etolle created by the sheer numbers of surfers.

For several years he rode his golden chariot over the sea, producing monstrous storms, attempting to drown out this invasion of his ocean. And while this method proved successful for most, it was not successful for all. Some of the surfers stayed with the steadily increasing size and violence of the waves created by Poseidon's chariot. They came to be surfers of such remarkable ability that their surfing skill came close to that of the slain Dylan.

Seeing that his efforts were eliminating most but strengthening others, Poseidon realized his error and sought to eliminate the manifestation in a different way: starvation. For hundreds of years the sea was calm as a sheet of glass. Whenever a ripple arose (a gull lifting off, a shooting star penetrating the surface like a bullet with a ts-s-s-s), Poseidon would rush there in an instant and calm the waters again. He became a lunatic about calmness. But in the end he lost control, and the reason he lost control was that he forgot about cycles and waves. Even his brother Zeus could not exist without (or even change) certain laws.

So it was that ninety-six centuries after Poseidon calmed the sea, the sea rose up and freed itself from his control. It was life or death—the oceans had to circulate (circles, cycles, waves), and not even Poseidon could stop that from occurring.

Meanwhile, the art of wave riding was being handed down from generation to generation in the form of various hidden formulae, sacred objects, and songs.

And people were riding more and more horses.

When the sea mutinied and began to pump again and was once again under the control of the cycles of the moon and the sun and the other forces of wave-generation, for a long time still no one surfed. It did not occur to them. It did not even occur to those who held fragments of the handed-down knowledge that the words, melodies, objects, and formulae they knew so well were in any way connected with the oceans and the waves.

"Where the inner, turning on itself, embraces the outer, there is the door to other worlds." This, they thought, referred to some distant idea of things that was of no practical value. Nor did they hear the sea in various resonant melodies, nor did they detect that same melody within themselves. Nor did the formula 8=8 cause them to pause. Abstract, they all thought. And no one noticed that the spear was the symbol of the surf-vessel that Dylan had given to man.

So it took a long time—some ninety-six more centuries—and then it was Poseidon himself (the only one who could actually remember) who yielded at last to an old temptation and departed his chariot to ride a spear within the waves, to taste what Dylan had offered. And those who saw most certainly marveled and tried to do it too (not knowing Poseidon was a god). But Poseidon was angered and turned on them to drive them off of his waves and out of his territory, and the ocean knew what might come of this and rose up and hurled Poseidon onto a coral reef in the Pacific where he was stung by a stone fish upon his Achilles tendon and perished.

It happened that among the Polynesians of those days, there were three men, each of whom contained a fragment of the secret knowledge. When news of the death of this god who rode the waves reached them, they all three sat in talk, and in the course of conversation, reflecting in the light of this new development, they simultaneously understood what it was they had been talking about, and what to do with those ancient spears.

At first the trio of Polynesians could not imagine engaging in such an activity. Sailing had taught them a huge respect for the oceans, and committing themselves to its waves upon such flimsy vessels was an insane concept to them. Yet it all fit, and someone—albeit a god—had already done it, and though he perished in the process, they were inspired to begin again, and the rest, at last, is history.

The introduction of competition—surfing contests—was an unavoidable complication, which for a long time has threatened to destroy the purity of this cosmic endeavor. Competition was not a part of it in the beginning; it came when the descendants of Lleu saw the descendants of Dylan riding the waves, and they were jealous.

Amazingly enough, in this present time of today, there are still pure descendants of the surfing school of Dylan, though they are almost totally invisible to the surfers descended from Lleu. Among other things, these descendants of the "Pure Art" (as it is called) don't generally communicate with those who have not been initiated. This initiation comes about through the blessed interaction with various mediatory elements. If you like, it can be made more specific.

I had not surfed in nineteen months. I was crawling along the ruins of the Coast Highway. I had forgotten who I was or where I was or if there was a who or where. I remember that the only thing turning around and around in my head was the idea that everything repeats. And this idea, as if to verify itself, kept repeating.

But I was aware that everywhere around me there were waves—the forests and hillsides, the clouds in the sky, the road—they were all waves. I did not, at the time, perceive nor conceive that there were forests, hillsides, clouds, or concrete. Only waves. The ocean, filled with waves, was like any of the other waves and seemed no more or less relevant to my situation, which at the time was extreme hunger.

I was an organic magnetic void, and I attracted what I beheld. A figure appeared, walking backward down the road towards me, dressed in flowing robes of shimmering scarlet, bathed in the electric waves of the sun's affection. I asked him where he was going, but of course he could only tell me where he had been; indeed, he was quite lucid in this regard. He told me that when he walked forward, he devoured the World, but since he had begun to walk backwards, the World now devoured him.

This struck a familiar chord in me. I blurted out that what he was experiencing might be similar to the Pure Art of Surfing and being in the curl of a wave. He looked at me oddly, then swept a hand over the scene around us (his scarlet robes billowing, gleaming) and said, "Which wave?"

"The ocean," I said. "Riding waves. Being inside. Coming out."

He asked me if I'd like to break my fast at his place. It was just there, he said, over the first dune, hidden by some long grass that grew on the sand like fur on a young rabbit. He shared his food with me, and then his friends came.

They were Riders of Waves, descended from the school of Dylan, they said. They told me that riding waves could be different for different people, that a person could only bring to it as much as he had and could only take from it as much as he could handle. If he took more, they said, he would lose it anyway and never know that he had lost anything, or had encountered the possibility of anything.

I asked them how they could ride waves differently, what it was that they meant by that. They said there was ancient knowledge concerning these possibilities, and that if you could find this knowledge you could begin to see what they meant, and later, as understanding grew, begin to ride waves in a different way, according to the Pure Art.

The surfers elucidated certain analogies of these possibilities. Some of these analogies were electrical.[2] Others were structural and mythological in nature.

"Surfing," they said, "has very deep mythological roots, but they have not been discovered by many men. And these mythologies are merely representations, allegories and clues to the great laws and possibilities that manifest with each wave. And everything is waves."

In spite of some nagging, deeper suspicions, I had always taken surfing to be essentially an exercise in free-release extra-effort fun. Now I was being told that there was something else in it. Some door to something greater, larger. "Does this door exist only in surfing?" I asked.

They said it was in everything, just as waves were in everything, though the vibrations—the frequency of wave production—are slower or faster in different media, making more or less energy available.

Then they showed me their "vessels"—their surfboards—and these were transparent, actually difficult to see in the soft light inside the bubble-house. I noticed that I was reluctant, even afraid to touch them—a fear of electrical shock—and when I did reach out and touch one, the moment vanished and "I" only appeared again when I removed my hand from it.

"These are Dylan's spears," I was told. "They would be of no use to you presently. Besides, you would have to reproduce your own. The fact that you could produce one of these vessels would show that you understood waves and the meaning of the Pure Art of Surfing."

I stayed with them that evening, I suppose. I did not remember myself again until I was somewhere well along the purple highway. I suddenly woke up to see that I was alone and still without a destination. I didn't know exactly where I was, but then I recalled being in that place for what seemed like a night. I realized that everything had changed, and I couldn't see how to change it back again. "Everything just happens," something in me said. "It's an endless perfection of waves. Again and again, it just happens, and there is no way to stop it. The art is in learning how to ride it, and the art is an attitude."

A very tall building crashed down in the distance, bringing me back to the road and the moment. Nearby, I could hear the sound of waves exploding onto a beach. I knew I had to get to them, but I also knew that I couldn't get to them in the old way, since there are no straight lines in nature.

There was a haze of smoke drifting across the road ahead. I seemed to remember all this happening before and that I had found the way then. So there was nothing to do but keep on until I found a place where the inner turned on itself to surround the outer—like the barrel of a wave—and then there would be a door.

ENDNOTES

1. "As we know from the study of undulatory vibrations in the world of physical phenomena, every wave comprises in itself a complete circle, that is, the matter of the wave moves in a completed curve in the same place and for as long as the force acts which creates the wave.

"We should know also that every wave consists of smaller waves and is in its turn a component part of a bigger wave.

"If we take, simply for the sake of argument, days as the smaller waves that form the bigger waves of years, then the waves of years will form one great wave of life. And as long as this wave of life rolls on, the waves of days and the waves of years must rotate at their appointed places, repeating and repeating themselves."

—Peter Ouspensky, *Tertium Organum: The Third Canon of Thought; A Key to the Enigmas of the World*; 2nd ed. rev., Alfred A. Knopf, New York, 1922.

2. The spiral of the wave was likened by them to an electromagnet creating a charged core. The surfer, in occupying the core space acts both as conductor and as transformer, turning this electrical energy (sprung negative ions) into physical and psychic energy. Thus, this energy need not all be lost, but can act as an energizing influence on the surfer who knows how to use it. From this we can see the appropriateness of the one-time popularity of the lightning bolt symbol on surfboards. It is a symbolic representation of a literal process.

This story first appeared in the December/January 1975–76 issue of Surfing *magazine and has been revised.*

heart of stone
(echoes of cultural shock)

MAY 1776

Palua

THE WILD DOGS WERE HOWLING in the hills, and the energy of the forest night rang within me. I was fifteen years old, out with my father and his three brothers. We had come for koa wood from which to make surfboards, and it was my first time. A rustling and a rummaging in the trees had awakened me to the distant crying of the dogs—*poki.*

Perhaps it was wild pigs that woke me, snorting and grumbling, anxious because their paths were scented with our human smell. Whatever it was, I lay there in the dark picturing it: the advancing bulge of deep water; the scooping, determined paddle to catch it; the sudden, gliding surge of motion; standing, turning, and facing the vertically erupting wall of liquid; and the streaking slide across the face towards the far-off channel, the curling falls looping over my head just ahead of me the whole way.

My mouth watered; it was the strongest craving that I had ever had: my own surfboard!

Only my father and uncles knew of this small, ancient valley on the side of Mauna Loa where huge koa grew. They had been taking their wood from a particular grove for forty years now; it was the best wood on the island of Hawai'i. We had come late the day before and had already selected a tree: a full, fat, hard koa with an evenness and symmetry, almost a calmness, about it. It dominated a large area of the grove and was clearly in its prime. My father and uncles had waited years for this night, and now it seemed as though I too had waited years for this night.

More thrashing in the brush startled me and woke one of my uncles, Kepapa. He woke Waiawa, Waimano, and my father, Manoa, with a single, sharp whisper. The five of us were wide awake and wide-eyed in the blackness as a commotion gathered around us then seemed to collect into a mass that began to circulate around our campsite in the night. The sound was like wind, or like a herd of creatures racing together in the brush, racing around and around us.

Yet its motion was soon so fast that it could no longer have been animals. It whirled faster and faster, whipping the air into motion. Suddenly we were in the middle of a whirlwind that threatened to suck us up into its fatal throat. We clawed at the earth for a hold. My father hooked an arm around me and held to a small wili-wili tree; my uncles grabbed what they could as I became stunned and transported by the realization that I could see them! The whirlwind was aglow!

But then the glow lifted and gathered high above our heads (showing us a huge, dark, spinning cone that whipped the mighty treetops as if they were young grass) and concentrated itself into a bright ball that grew tense and somehow brittle, then exploded outwards in a jagged shaft of lightning that shot off into the grove of koa.

And then all was calm, twigs and branches raining down amid a gentle fall of leaf. In the distance the wild dogs had stopped their howling.

In the morning, having slept poorly, Waimano groaned aloud that the work of cutting such a huge tree was more than he wished to undertake. And then the long trek to the village with four hundred pounds of wood! We others sighed sympathetically as we started off into the grove.

How strange it was to first sense some vacancy in the sky, some hollowness and absence and unfamiliarity. Manoa gave a start, spoke a few words quickly in a low voice: "Wait! Something powerful has been at work here!" Our pace became a creeping as we slipped silently into the once-shadowed domain of the great koa. Now it lay half out of its world, its weight crushing down upon several smaller trees. It had been severed cleanly at the base; some earth had even been plowed up at the roots by the impact: the lightning!

The cut was pure and uncharred, as if the stab of electric fire had been cold.

Much of the work had been done for us, and after placing the ceremonial red kumu fish at the base of the trunk, we set to work with our tools about four arm-spans up the trunk. We worked in total silence, only the sound of our hacking as there was much energy in the place and a definite fear that we were being too bold in taking our wood from a tree touched by the gods.

Past noon we had cut off our length, severed it from the rest, and rolled it out into the clearing. We ate passion fruit and nuts, then set to work once more, dividing the log lengthwise in order to take out the planks for two surfboards.

It was another night and a day to accomplish this, so hard was the wood, and when at last the two parts broke apart, there was a large, clear, red stone caught up inside the wood that popped free. This left a sizeable depression in each side, like the sockets of two eyes, except that there had been only one eye.

We trimmed the halves down and made them manageable for the trail. A hole was hollowed in the stump of the fallen tree, and another kumu placed in it as an offering. Then worship was made to the gods that we had in those days.

One more night we stayed, all completed, then started down early the third morning, two men to each plank, and me behind with the tools and provisions and the transparent red stone.

We came down out of the mountains at sunset and across the open space towards the huts of our village. Everyone stopped their doings to race out and greet us with their delighted and curious faces. My father greeted them in return with a smile, but soon grew more serious.

"The gods have touched these," he said, indicating the two fine slices of koa. "We do not know our fate for bringing them down here." He said that it would be best if no one else were to touch them, and the five of us continued on to my father's canoe house, leaving our friends and relatives chattering noisily behind us.

JUNE 1776
Manoa

When the right day came we made offerings in the *heiau* and asked the gods to guide our surfboards and bless us with great waves. Then we set them into the water, called on the Great Shark to be a worthy ally, and I and my son, Palua, made our way out to the surf. The boards were gleaming bright in the sun. We had taken every possible care in their construction. They were shaped as if born from the most perfect shark: worried into perfection in my canoe house with the honed edges of the finest adzes, worked smooth with coral sanding blocks, buffed flawless with oil stone, then rubbed and polished with kukui nut oil. More perfect surfboards had never been seen, so far as we could tell. Yet both still bore the socket left by the imprint of the stone, and in this hole, on both boards, I had carved a bolt of lightning: a reminder of that night. The surfboards were named Pali and Paliki, and we were given fine waves to ride on that first day.

Already, just from paddling out to *kulana nalu* (the lineup), we knew the surfboards were sleek and fast, as they whispered through the water without resistance.

And then, as if by chance, we were far outside, getting the feel of them, when a huge wave arose that somehow we were perfectly positioned for. I and Palua slid down its great face together.

Never had there been two surfboards like these. I was taken by a moment of fright when I first tasted their great speed and looked to Palua, fearing that he might be out of control. But his face was the mirror of such great thrill and pleasure that I myself was set at ease, and we flew across the long and hollow wall together, continually eluding the efforts of the wave to trap us.

DECEMBER 1776
Palua

That morning in December of 1776, I awoke with a start to hear a remarkable, and deep-throated thunder. In an instant, as the sleep rolled off me like warm water, I knew that it was the sea. The night before the water had gone incredibly calm and a great heaviness was everywhere. People in our village were subdued and pensive, and even the children played quietly among themselves, occasionally looking up and around, troubled.

That morning, after climbing to the top of the headland, I was wrapped in a great mist. The sun was shining, yet there were only faint shadows, so much water was in the air. Pu'u, at the outside of Keolanahihi Bay, was breaking four times the usual distance from shore, and, to me, the waves looked to be a hundred feet tall, and the explosions of their breaking were like eruptions from the volcanoes at Mauna Loa.

As I stood there my father and Kepapa were suddenly beside me, looking out at this most unbelievable surf. After awhile I saw them look at one another and I saw that some sort of agreement sounded between them without words or visible signs. My father turned to me.

"We will need Paliki," he said. I looked at my Uncle Kepapa. That surfboard was, of course, my dearest possession beyond a doubt. Yet what was I to do? I knew full well that it was not even necessary for my father, or even Kepapa for that matter, to ask me. I nodded, and abruptly they turned and were moving quickly down the winding trail back towards the huts.

Soon I saw them enter the water on the far side of the headland. They had picked a good lull and the boards were the swiftest paddlers known, almost as fast as a twenty-man war canoe. For a long time I watched them, and finally they appeared, only after long intervals, rising over the tops of the monstrous waves. Then they were too far and I could not see them at all. By this time most of the village had heard that the surf was being challenged, and people filled the headland. There was much concern for the lives of my father and uncle, and even some betting between Makini, the odds-maker, and various men of the village.

The sets began to come without interval, steadily and around the same size. Manakoa said that they were seven men high and others nodded agreement. A group of women sat on the hillside chewing awa root, and spitting its potent extraction into a huge wooden bowl. Their eyes were wide and vacant and they took no notice at all of the proceedings.

Suddenly a cheer went up! Outside two white tracks marked the descent into the trough of one of the huge waves. For a long way the wakes were drawn into and over with the lip of the mighty wave. They seemed to be making it well, although we could not see them. Their track looked good for the bowl before the channel. And then the face that was curling over was clean of any marks. A great Ooooooooo! went up and a stirring and worrying took hold of us.

A long time we waited, then finally an object appeared out in front of one of the broken waves, bounced and pushed ahead of it: a man prone upon a surfboard. But was it my father or my uncle: A panic began to creep over me and it was a great effort to control myself and wait till the surfer had passed the headland and was skittering towards the steep eroding beach.

It was Manoa, my father. And there was something new in his eyes that day. He was not the same thereafter.

Long, long we waited on the beach for my uncle and my surfboard to return, but they did not return that day, nor did they return the next, nor the next. At sunset of the third day my father called me down from the roof where I had been thatching in new palm.

"Palua," he said. "Your uncle has not returned and will not now return. So also your *papa he'e nalu* (surfboard) will not be coming back to you. Both have been taken by the waves. Your father wearies over his error in judgment by attempting too great a feat. He has decided that his *olo* is now yours, hoping that you will know your opponent better than he knew his."

Seldom was I to use the great *olo* surfboard. Indeed, in some parts of the island it would be unlawful for me even to have one, as we were *makaainana*, commoners, not the royal *Ali'i*. Yet it was a joy to know that it was there, carefully wrapped in clean tapa, waiting for the time when it would be needed. Meanwhile I rode my short *alaia* on the snappy little waves that broke off the point around the headland.

And one day, perhaps two months after the disappearance of my uncle, as I stopped to pick up my board where it had washed ashore, there was a chunk of koa wood on the sand, a finely finished piece with a scooped-out depression in it, and in the depression was the familiar, jagged lightning bolt.

May 1778
Kaimoku

I remember it as if it were yesterday. Palua and I were surfing beautiful shoulder-high waves at Pau Nihi, the point around the headland from our village. The waves were extremely fast, crisp, and hollow; *kakala nalu hai lalas*, we called them. The day was windless and unusually glassy, even into the afternoon. The sun beat down fiercely, and there had been sharks out beyond the *kulana nary* a couple of times that morning.

Lilikala, on the beach making *ilima leis*, would jump to her feet when one of us had a good ride. We could hear her sparkling voice across the water, though it was embarrassing for both Palua and myself, as we were best friends and were both in love with Lilikala, the most beautiful girl in the village.

After one particularly nice ride, in which Palua spent a long time standing on the front of the board in the grip of the hollow wave, he paddled in and gave me the torment of observing the two of them playing on the beach, touching one another, and laughing. I could only watch for a short time before I frantically paddled for a wave and hastened in towards shore. Once there, of course, I felt foolish.

"In so soon, Kaimoku?" teased Palua with a sly look.

I turned and looked out at the break and a perfect five-footer. I faced them again, red-cheeked.

"Yes, well, I thought it was losing its shape."

"You mean you were losing your shape," Palua laughed.

I could not take my eyes off of Lilikala, nor be unaware that one of Palua's fingers idly touched her foot where it lay in the white sand.

What were we to do, I wondered?

Precisely at that moment there was the reverberating sound of the village conch, calling an emergency assembly. We left our surfboards where they lay, and Palua and I each took one of Lilikala's hands and we all raced off to see what the commotion was about. We ran up the backside of the headland and reached the top panting for breath.

Below, the village was gathered on the beach, and the war canoes were being launched as well as every available outrigger and surfboard. We looked out to sea then and saw a most marvelous and unforgettable sight: three great, white sailing birds swept across the waters just outside of our bay. They appeared to be the personal canoes of the gods, perhaps of the Sun God himself, I did not know. But how magnificently they moved! How unaffected by the swells that passed beneath them, while our canoes dipped and plunged out of the bay.

Then we were running north along the coastal trail, me and Palua, and there was a roar of excitement bursting down in my throat as we ran along with the mighty vessels of the gods.

We ran all the way to Makahoa Bay and the village there. Although we could have, and would have, run further if needed, the huge, winged canoes turned into the bay and we were soon on the beach with a flood of others, hoping for a space in a canoe. But we were outsiders with last priority, and soon we were in the water swimming out to meet our masters and saviors. About this time the first of the war canoes from our village rounded the headland, the rowers rocking in a frantic rhythm, and all at once hundreds of boats converged upon the three great apparitions. And there upon the high decks looking down at us were the white-faced beings of another world, calling to us in an unintelligible tongue.

"Are you gods?" we called. "Are you the Sun Gods?" But they could not understand us, nor we them, and we soon realized that of course our gods would be able to speak so that we could understand them.

JANUARY 1826
Palua

So many had died by this time, so many of our people invisibly struck down by the poisons of the Europeans. And now there were these missionaries, making huts of wood in which to give praise to their "god" and in which our children were taught the knowledge and ways of another world.

Only a few of us surfed like we used to. Kaimoku would sometimes come. Lilikala and the children came too, to play on the beach, and sometimes she would tandem with me, but now we had to watch out and be careful. The missionaries became angry if we did not wear tapa or cloth. Some even became angry at our surfing. "Idleness!" they said, and "sport of the devil." The devil was the force of evil that they gave to us, then told us we had to drive him out. It was like a game of tag.

Palakiki still rode his surfboard, though lately he had taken up the practice of shooting an American gun. He was once *Ali'i*, but not any longer. Now there were just *naka'ainanas*.

Many ships had come to the big bays to the north by now, and though their Captain Cook was killed a long time ago at Kealakekua, that did not stop them.

But the ways of these Europeans were harmful and fatal to people such as we were then, and I, for one, would not be changed by their customs and threats.

OCTOBER 1838
Páki

My father, Palua, is growing very old, and yet he does not seem to grow tired of trying to persuade me to take up his great old *olo* and ride the surf as he did when he was a young man. Yes, and he still surfs the smaller waves on occasion, though he is in his seventies now.

But for me the learning I have received from the missionaries is immensely more valuable than the old-time play of sentimental grandfathers.

Already I am prepared for a fine job: a sugar mill is being built back of Kolaoa, and I can have a clerical job if I have a suit of new clothes to wear.

Besides, the thatched huts and surfboards and *heiau* temples of the past are nothing compared to the fantastic world that will someday be created on these very islands. And, as I have often assured my father, surfing will be of no significance to the greater things of life. Why, already they are bringing in the Chinese and the Japanese to work in the huge new mills. And surfing is rarely seen around here any more. You cannot have surfing without children and young men, I tell my father. And most of the children and young men are dead.

"What about you?" my father challenges when I speak of this to him. "You are a young man," he says.

"I'm thirty-eight," I tell him, "and the waves are nothing to me."

DECEMBER 1840
Palua

Lilikala is dead now. The children have died or have gone off to missionary school and died in a different way. Nothing. Nothing anymore.

I look back on it. There was so much. It seems now that there is so little of it left.

I don't know what to do now. I could go back up into that koa grove and wait. Perhaps I could return the red stone and maybe it will be taken up once again into another great-hearted tree. Or I could stay here and wait. There is little else to do now.

DECEMBER 1840
Páki

To me it was madness, simply the senility of an old man wandering in the mist of his memories. Surfing a three-foot wave would have been foolish at his age, but Pu'u was said to be forty feet.

"He rode well!" they all say. So what? He's dead all the same and left me nothing. Or almost nothing. Strange about that piece of koa . . . It washed up on the beach, right at my feet, hours after he was gone. And I took it up to his hut and found another there, identical to it. And lightning carved in a hollow of each piece. And then that strange red stone that he had always had. How squarely it set in the sockets of koa . . . almost as if, in the middle of a great tree . . .

But no, I begin to sound like he did, and if I am to succeed in this brave new Hawai'i, I must remember the future, not the past.

This story first appeared in the February/March 1975 issue of Surfing *magazine.*

the island

THE VILLA V_____ IS OWNED and operated by Herr and Frau G. In October and November of 1968, many of the competitors in the World Contest stayed here, living in the quaint, neat cabins that are interspersed throughout the jungle-like garden of their properties.

One especially dark, rich evening, I followed the curving drive to their house, walked over the humpbacked wooden bridge that straddles a kind of moat surrounding the Big House, and came to the door of the screened-in porch. The smell of incense, the sound of soft piano music, and a soft, suggestive amber light flowed out into the darkness. I knocked on the frame of the screen door, and the vibration chased several large moths into the air. They fluttered around briefly, brushing my face and thumping the screens, before settling again on the wire mesh, stuck there like Chinese rice-paper cuttings.

It seemed a long time before someone came to the door: a tall, severe-looking man in khaki shorts and short-sleeved white shirt, short-cropped gray-white hair, and steel-rimmed spectacles.

"Yes?" he asked in a soft, yet somehow dominating voice, standing back three or four feet from the door. I introduced myself and said that I was staying in such-and-such a cabin and asked if I could use the telephone to call collect to my office in California. He seemed a bit suspicious of me still, so I added that Frau G. had checked me in earlier that afternoon. He undid a hook and pushed out on the screen door. He held it open until I'd entered a large porch area with woven-mat carpeting, wicker furniture, oil lamps, driftwood, and huge, perfect shells. He showed me into the next room, a small alcove off the kitchen, and pointed to the telephone. I noticed Frau G. in yet another room; she looked up from her reading, but showed no sign of recognition.

I tried to make my phone call, but needed help from Herr G. with the unfamiliar Puerto Rican telephone service. I reached California, told Severson what was happening (swell on the way down, the contest extremely disorganized, the island beautiful) and received instructions. As I talked, I casually glanced over a framed chart of the local waters that was hung on the wall above the desk where I sat.

After I had hung up and Herr G. had returned and was standing there waiting to show me out, I asked him about the waves off his beach. He pointed out that the coastline turned to face somewhat to the southwest here and that there were seldom swells to disturb the lake-like calm. He showed me where we were on the map.

I asked him about a small island that was on the map about four inches from the Villa V_____. I had seen the sun go down just south of it that evening and had been attracted to it for some reason, or maybe for no reason.

His response was strange: he asked me in an extremely odd way why I wanted to know about "the island." I sort of laughed and said I didn't know, I was just kind of curious about it because I'd noticed it at sunset.

"No one goes out to the island," he said.

"Do you know if there are any good waves out there?" I asked.

"What do you mean?" he said.

"I was just wondering if there might be good places to surf off the island," I said.

"Why would you want to go out to the island to ride your waves? There are plenty of waves at the point of Rincon and at the nuclear point and on the north shore; you can surf there."

After I'd said good night and walked back across the bridge, my thoughts returned again to the island. I'd just asked out of curiosity and hadn't had any thoughts about going out there, but now I was interested and wanted to know more.

Over the next couple of weeks, I gathered information on the island. I talked to fishermen and surfers and townsfolk. I heard a wide variety of interesting stories. Some said the island was used as a military target; bombing missions were run from the nearby air base, and the island was a desolation of craters. Others said there were perfect waves off the north and south points, and that at the south, a right and a left converged into a huge wedge wave often over thirty feet high. Others said that some fishermen lived there and would come in periodically to sell their take. Still others asserted that there was a family of young people out there who surfed and who were avoiding the draft and the war in Vietnam. Then there was a recurring and weird tale that the island was overrun by monkeys, thousands of them, and that the monkeys (according to some sources) had an intelligent leader, and this was why basically no one lived there (and also why the island was a bombing target).

Eventually, the island became a psychological backdrop to the events of the day—surfing with Nat Young and Midget Farrelly and this hot-little-kid-with-the-space-needle-surfboard named Reno Abellira; evenings at the Villa V____, pulling urchins out of hands and feet while waiting for dinner to be served; heading up to Punta Higuera for the mornings, to Domes for the afternoons, to Rincon for the evenings; and the island lurking out there near the sunken sun . . .

Finally, the World Contest ended, and the surfers left Puerto Rico. The stories were written, and the secrets were made known: there were good waves, tropical conditions, palm trees, exotic fruit, and inexpensive living just $90 from the mainland. Over the intervening years, every hot East Coast surfer has put in his journeyman apprenticeship on Puerto Rico's snappy, occasionally gnarly, surf.

Since then, the sun has set three thousand times out by the island. Today it costs a lot more to surf out on the western end of Puerto Rico. The waves are more crowded, and the local people have certain attitudes about surfers that were not in their smiling faces when the first of us came.

The Villa V____ is still there, and Herr and Frau G. are there, too, although the good Frau G. now manages the whole affair with the assistance of Roderigo. Herr G. is almost totally paralyzed. He sits all day long now behind the screens of the large veranda in an old wicker wheelchair, looking out, perhaps nodding. They will not rent to surfers any more because of damage done to their property over the years, but I presented myself to them as just a tourist (my board at Rudolfo's in Rincon under the house) and had no problem.

Ironically, when Frau G. showed me to my cabin it turned out to be the one I had wanted the last time, but it had been rented then. It was right on the beach, looking out past the black rock towards the island. I was astonished that I still found that island so compelling; I missed several sentences of Frau G.'s presentation watching the blue-gray clouds swarm around its abrupt heights. I had to see it.

I spoke with Herr G. two nights later. Although it was late, he was still on the veranda in the wheelchair; the years had shrunken him. He looked almost like an elderly monkey with spectacles, though he seemed emotionally softer than before, perhaps because of his intense sufferings. I was sure that he would not remember me; it had been over eight years. But as soon as I asked about the island, he knew, and maybe he knew before that, because he said:

"Why do you still talk about the island? Forget island."

The next day I rented a boat out of Mayaguez and headed towards the island. The day was clear and bright and yet there was a darkness—where the sun is so bright and the clouds so absent that everything seems to be in shade. The surface of the channel was a fine chop, and there were swells and occasional fins, though I'm not sure whether they were porpoise or shark or both. The island is about twenty-five miles out. About five miles from it, I could see whitewater all around the south point. From this distance, it was clear that the island was simply a mountain peak. There was no beach along its east shore, and just a long spit of sand came off the south. To the north as far as I could see the island plunged straight into the depths of the ocean.

There were large ledges and plateaus higher on the island. There were many palms that came into focus from about two miles out. The waves peeled off the southern tip at about fifteen feet. Steam shot out of the empty barrels as I closed in. My stomach was fluttery because I was alone, I suppose, and also because I was afraid of big surf, especially in a new place. I shut off the engine about a quarter mile outside the break and listened to it and watched it. It was definitely grinding and sounded like the waves were composed of round boulders rolling over each other.

I stood in the rocking boat and took it all in knowing that I wasn't going to try to surf the waves. During the lulls, a strange sound came off the island, as if some great invisible activity were occurring. Just when I would start to identify the sound, the sets would start roaring through again and drown it out.

I gradually became more and more unsettled and finally felt quite an unreasonable fear. I began to worry that I might run out of gas or that I would be unable to start the engine again. This last thought made my spine prickle, so I tried the starter. Nothing. I tried again, and it kicked over.

I had just throttled forward when a cool gust of wind blew over me from the island carrying with it a scent that made my skin crawl. I do not know how to describe it except to say that it was the smell of something living, and not in the sense that a jungle is living or animals are living. There was an odor at once evil and intelligent.

I swung the boat around hard and made back for Mayaguez. I didn't turn again for about two miles, and when I did there was a piercing stab of white light from the peak of the island, as if someone were signaling with a mirror. I turned my back on it and opened the throttle full-bore.

The rest of Puerto Rico was fine: all the sweets of the good surfing life, the pretty ladies down the lane, and all that. Herr G. sat all day (and maybe all night) behind the screens. I wondered if maybe he hadn't had a good sniff of that island once. In any case, I never asked him about it again.

This story originally appeared under the title "Puerto Rico, My Heart's Devotion" in the October/November 1977 issue of Surfing *magazine.*

beyond the green diamonds

HE LAY BLOATED AND PALE like a soaked rag just out of reach of the ocean's white fingers.

A small circle of people surrounded him, some shivering and dripping, red-faced and chattering, others bundled in sweaters and slacks and tennis shoes, watching, whispering. A small, quick laugh was muted by the slight whip of the early morning wind in the damp air. Out over the water, white gulls chased in and out of the offshore fog: watching, wings whispering . . .

It had been a long night, and Ray Stickles might have given the whole of it a great deal of thought, except that he was lying there, the axis of a small circle, full of saltwater and the sediment of muted screams. He was, the small circle of people had finally decided, quite dead. But if he wasn't dead, if he wasn't lying like a fish just dragged from the sea, still beating the sand indignantly, outraged, still able to think, then, if he were alive, he would think back on his last very long night. Think back to . . .

Sitting solitary and cold in the yellow presence of the small light in the back of his VW bus, sitting, watching the drizzle spatter the view from his window—watching the water streak the blackness of the outside into reflections of himself beside the yellow glare of the light, and beyond the reflections the white explosions of waves in the black void—fingering the capsule of LSD and wondering whether he would take it here, now, alone. Wondering: was there anything else to do? Sitting there alone and damp, cold, waiting for morning and surf, he cocked back his head and dropped the capsule into his mouth and swallowed.

Alone, as he had ever been alone, watching out the dappled window at black nothingness, listening to the rain, like blown sand, scatter over the roof, listening to the breathing roar and hiss of the functioning ocean, Ray Stickles sat waiting to be taken out of his condition, waiting while the capsule dissolved away in his stomach, pulsed into his blood, inflated his veins and arteries, and refracted and twisted his mind much in the same way that the mist refracted and twisted the world beyond the window.

He reached over into the front seat and pulled his portable radio from under the dash. He turned it on and hung it by the strap from the window latch, listening to the warbling static that came from somewhere in the black swamp beyond the distorted glass telling him that even if he were in debt or had been arrested or had been refused credit by everyone else—even then, the voice attested, fighting in a pool of static, even then, we—yes, we alone—will give you credit. Somehow, though, Ray Stickles, sitting alone and cold, was not noticeably warmed by the anonymous message of good cheer. Fumbling with thought and hungering for someone to talk to, for some sort of communication, for some straw of contact to grab on to, Ray Stickles reached out for something to pull him through the night. Then the acid began to warp the prism of his mind, and the first glancing blows of bent light beat at his eyes.

Waiting, his stomach grew heavy and his breathing labored against the pull of muscles he had never felt before. His pulse quickened, and the yellow light in the roof of the Kombi glowed mellow and became so warm that, holding his hands to the light, they seemed to lose their cold, damp stiffness. He began to relax, viewed the drifting part of himself as a separate entity. Each blob of water on the window became a warm, crystal pearl, and the reflection of himself and the inside of the bus with the yellow light became as warped and unreal as the water made the world beyond the glass appear. He relaxed into a new security, thinking along with the recorded static: Relax, turn off your mind, and float upstream. Ray Stickles began to think he had it made.

He threw open the side doors of the Kombi and stepped down into the sand, sinking, it seemed, nearly to his knees. But the sand seemed warm and soft, so he continued on into it, slogging off from the bus, feeling the warm, buffeting night wind, hearing its deep rumble in his ears, feeling the swell and rush of the wind around him.

A new pulse struck a rhythm in his mind, but he realized almost immediately that it was Dylan, distant now, through the static: "The country music station plays soft, but it's nothing, really nothing to turn off . . ." Exactly! Ray

Stickles thought, and let the static continue because it really wasn't anything to turn off, or even to listen to. It was merely a new, different pulse—the pulse of the electric spasm that shudders forever through the entire world. Nothing. Really nothing.

He danced slowly down the beach, spinning, his whole being rushing in a seasick swirl while he moved slowly till the warm sea churned delicately around his ankles, beckoning. Then, turning, he caught the golden reflection from the side of the bus that scattered itself on the wet sand by the sea. He looked up and saw the gigantic monster that had been the bus, its huge, fire-heaped mouth opened to swallow until, watching, he saw it slither towards him across the sand, moving without motion, approaching without approach, coming without effort, by force of gravity, somehow, alone, until the beast was on him, above him, and finally within him, and he lost consciousness.

When he blinked awake in the gray dawn, the beast had returned to its place within the bus, and Ray Stickles found that he still stood beside the sea. He thought of how he had really freaked now, and noted, too, the sense of pride that followed the realization.

The sea was gray but inviting, almost beckoning, to him. He slogged heavily back to the bus and stripped and slid into his fiery red trunks and opened the back of the bus and drew out his board from the overhead racks. The board was unusually heavy and cumbersome in his arms; and, as he stooped to wax it, the relief map of months of wax danced three-dimensionally before him, raised a few inches from the board's surface. He rubbed carefully back and forth, feeling his muscles pull against movement, his stomach harden. In the water and paddling, Ray Stickles had trouble keeping centered on the board. He found the swells lifted him in strange arcs, held him at weird angles; sometimes he held his board sideways, his feet angling into a magnetized void many miles deep. Yet instincts built up of years of surfing pulled him mechanically out into the lineup where the sea, like blue skin, ruptured upwards from rippling tendons, and waves were formed. After what seemed to be weeks, he was alone in the lineup. All this and still alone and still, beneath all the mental riot, still reaching for the straw that would conduct communication from himself to someone other than himself. He was still alone.

Alone until, wrapped in the silk of motion, the part of him that had been taught through the years to respond, did, indeed, respond and flailed wildly at the water till both halves of his being were catapulted forward on the surfboard and instinct snatched back its power from hallucination. A long drop, a bottom turn and three climbs and drops, and instinct was the master—for the moment. But just after the final climb and drop, he trimmed smoothly and his mind, the hallucinating half of his being, caught on the steadily building wall of crystal and green diamonds. He was cutting across the side of a huge pile of uncut diamonds, and he saw his withered face in each of them; and in each of them, his withered face turned away; and he watched them until he saw the nose of his board dip into the green stones. He waited, watching, for the nose to resurface; and then a lapse, and he was in the warm jelly of sweet saltwater, calling out for a straw to grab at, for some communication, for someone to talk to besides the freak within himself.

The circle dissolved almost immediately with the sound of the siren. Those that didn't wish to be involved gathered their sweaters around their necks and trudged off, whispering. The wet, dripping ones cast a common eye on the approaching ambulance. Out over the water, a pair of white gulls bent in and out of the dense offshore fog, watching, wings whispering.

This story originally appeared in the July 1968 issue of Surfer *magazine.*

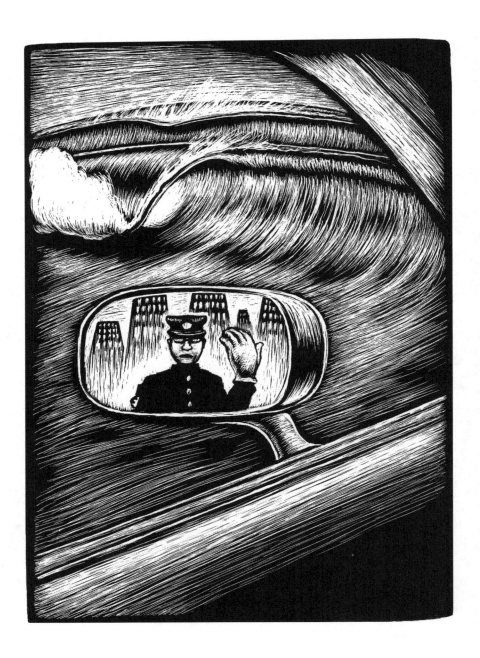

interruptions in a continuing story

GENTLY BACKWARDS . . . A GROUP OF THEM coming out of the fog in Nineteen Sixty. Voices counterpointing in the close press of the gray mist . . . muffled . . . until . . . bursting into sunlight:

"Swear t'god man. Swear t'god. I counted to six an' then he ate his lunch."

There was a cold, white silence standing now in the new sun as they contemplated the feat. It drove them into hopelessness that the Master could do for six seconds what they could only fake.

"Right *on* the tip?"

"Toes over."

"Shit."

They settled down into the warm sand of the pit. Malibu was four feet. Late September.

They stretched out on the heavy Hawai'ian sand, too, near the huge sucking throat of the rip at Sunset Beach. They sat in the sun, turning brown in the heat, feeling unsettled and driven and faintly aware that the ocean seemed to be filling with surfers who were never there before.

"It's big."

"So what?"

"It's *too* big."

"It's never too big."

Yes, and California is gutless compared. One thing to surf with friends. Another to surf alone, among crowds. A subtle game of dominance. But who's ready for the big step? What good's your mainland ego out there? A higher, more sophisticated, and more dangerous game was developing. A new kind of one-upmanship—a game for endless appetites—and there were players who needed to be on top.

He was, indeed, a hopeless case. Out of the Midwest and old at seventeen as a result of his parents' shifting life (his father a bird colonel, always moving). Paralyzed by motion (no use unpacking if you've just got to pack again), he kept himself in traveling form. Lived out of his suitcase, so to speak. Never opened up, nor put down roots, nor made real friends. Traveling form.

Because this was the way it was, the way he seemed to be, he thought of himself as a stone bumping through a forest, rolling always on, collecting little in the way of moss, and living inside himself like a stone does. And when he struck a tree, made contact in the ever-night, the tree could feel him, would ever be bruised by his unyielding impact. Yet he could never feel the tree and was only faintly aware that his course had been altered.

His name was Benjamin Thayer, and his life was a closed and secret place, feeding off itself in cannibalistic fashion, until the day he discovered surfing.

He came over the hill and down to the sea, and there was surfing, right there in the Pacific Ocean, where, as far as he knew, it had been practiced since infinity began.

Benjamin began to surf. In a frenzy he paid seventy-five dollars for a five-year-old Dave Sweet surfboard, tied it to the roof of his father's new Pontiac, and headed to where the surfing was. The dented skin of the old board, scraped clean for resale, was as slippery as the back of some huge, scaleless fish until a more experienced surfer, paddling by his thrashing form, gave him the loan of a sandy piece of wax.

Soon he came to feel secure proned-out upon the rough deck of the blue board. He could paddle over swells without sliding off; he could turn the board by flailing both hands in the cold, gray-green water and let the boiling rush of a broken wave fold icily over him—and sometimes it caught him just right and carried him chattering towards shore, just out ahead of the ragged white line. And he would grip the edges of the board in his two numb hands and strain to keep the nose from pearling and look from side to side at the bubbling soup.

One time he tried to stand, got as far as his knees, and rolled over to one side. Soon after he made it to his feet, but was standing too far back and fell off the tail and had to swim to the shore for the board. He thought of this as his first wipeout.

For a long time after he had learned to catch broken waves he would stand and the board would pearl. He would watch helplessly as the tip jammed inexorably under the fine, unforgiving line of surface. He had to watch other surfers before he became aware of the necessity for a rocking, fluid rhythm that kept the board responding to the rider. He found that the board could not surf by itself.

Benjamin Thayer became a surfer in the early Sixties. He surfed four or five days a week, weekends, and after school. When school became college he cut classes whenever there was a chance of surf. He came to know other surfers, was even on speaking terms with some of them. And knowing them he realized that they were human, and being human, he realized, meant that he could outsurf them.

Because if there was one thing that Benjamin had going for him it was that he never started anything he didn't have the energy to carry through perfectly to the end.

Persistently, inevitably, he became very good; and then he was hot. He entered contests and won. People began to know who he was. He started riding for a Santa Monica surfboard manufacturer. He became their Number One rider. He became Number One in the United States Surfing Association. He was bold, aggressive, and radical in the water. He learned to outfox and dominate a crowd of hungry surfers. He became the center of the real world and thought that everyone either loved or hated him, feared or respected him.

Everyone who he knew he knew through surfing, and therefore everyone who he knew was a competitor of his. He was a very good competitor and therefore better than everyone he knew. He assumed that all these persons respected him because of his ability and because he did not openly hate them except in the water. In the end he had a bit of money and a bit more fame, but no friends. And in his heart raged a fire that could not be fed, and could not be put out.

"Ooooooorainy night and who but me would . . . would . . . I . . . some . . . well . . . just me . . . need to see if I . . . I can want . . . to be me . . . walking here . . . in here . . . away from being here . . . gotta get where I'm going . . . I gotta . . .

gotta get alone . . . just me . . . see if I can be me here . . . in here . . . walking away
. . . need want to have got I alone me needing walking from being would . . . would
. . . would . . . who but me oooooorainy night . . . " Benjamin thought.

A VW bus parked beside the fire hydrant on PCH. Two long-time Malibu surfers
sit in the opened side doorway with a sign advertising Free Coffee & Do-Nuts, the
sign propped against the hydrant. Out in the water, a contest is happening.

"Sorry, for contestants only."

"Here y'are."

"Thanks."

"Don't mention it."

When most of the top guys in the semifinal have been supplied, the two dudes
close up the doors and start up the bus, turning on the windshield wipers till the
parking ticket flies off and flutters like time back along the Coast Highway.

"Where to?"

"Arabia."

With the coming of the Vals, the old surfers pulled up stakes and moved on. No
one knew where, really. Some split to the Islands, which held out for a while.
Some moved on to Australia. Some to Europe. Some to South Africa. Some . . .

They left behind a whole new generation of anxious, aggressive kids riding
waves that were shadows of a long-gone glory that was never there. Like a swarm
of mountain yellow jackets come to cart off pieces of flesh.

Alone again in the full world. Benjamin first struck out in anger against the
people around him. He grew sour and hostile and downright antagonistic. He
blamed and hated everyone for his alienation. But in the end he came to the
inevitable, and he struck out, or in, against himself.

Because he saw in a flash where he was, and it shook him to the base
of his soul. He saw the layers upon layers of falsehood that shrouded that
cold, clear mystery at the very heart of him: that pure white untouched energy
that was imprisoned there by all the guises of his ego—the responsibility and

concomitant dread of existence.

He felt the stab of the sun, felt himself being sucked forever onwards, forever out of control, flailing all the way into infinity. And at last he saw the meaning of the words Flow With It.

It was at a Malibu Contest. Somebody had put acid in the donuts.

Benjamin turned in circles. He walked around city blocks, around parked cars, around revolving doors, around and around other people. Though essentially restrained, he felt his energy mounting, building. Soon it would blossom out like cauliflower, and he would veer off on his new direction.

He peeled away at the artichoke of himself. Tearing off leaves, sampling what flesh was there, and tearing off more leaves. Searching for the heart of it.

He gave up surfing. The environment out in the water had become too negative. Everyone competing with everyone else. There was no true brotherhood. No true love of man. People would have to change if the world was ever going to be straightened out. Before it was too late. Or else.

Benjamin took a lot of acid. He learned to do yoga. He composed his own mantra. He studied his stars, cast the *I Ching*, studied his numerology, and had his palm read. Everywhere he was destined for Greatness. He would, perhaps, be a leader in this new brotherhood thing. He could help people get it together. If he only had the energy.

Benjamin began to take speed, then cocaine, then smack. He filled his veins full of every imaginable chemical, and in the end he was still going in circles, but much faster.

Well, said Benjamin one day, so much for that. He said it every time he came around. So much for that.

"This is it?" the first Malibu surfer asked.

"Yeah," the second Malibu surfer nodded. "This is it."

"What now."

"We wait."

"For what?" the first asked.

"Just wait."

It happened in the morning and peaked as the day crested beneath a hard noon sun. Benjamin knew what it was he had to do. He had to move . . . get away.

He sold all that he owned and gave away what he couldn't sell. He said good-bye to his girlfriend:

"Good-bye, Earth Woman."

"Good-bye, Benbow."

He went and stood where the pit once was at Malibu and saw the lifeguard tower at second point and the two crescent-shaped arcs of the point that were once rounded nearly into one before all that rain that year. He watched guys with elastic plastic leashes wearing full-length wetsuits and booties and paranoid faces waggling and jerking all over three-foot waves. And in his heart Benjamin puked the puke of the soul that comes to all true Benjamins sooner or later.

"Howzit, Benj," someone said.

"Hey," said Benjamin, watching the guy's back as he walked down onto the flat of the beach, headed for the third point beachbreak.

"No use to fight might right got to got to gotta get outta being here and now and get there while the gettin's good gotta gotta move on out a sight and gotta gotta do it NOW! . . . " Benjamin thought.

He had a fat roll of bills with a rubber band around it. He could go anywhere. Do anything. But . . .

But there was fear in his soul. Paranoia and claustrophobia of large caliber demanding immediate remedy, immediate relief. Immediate movement.

He took a plane to the Islands. He wrestled with a low-hanging, black cloud all the way over; even spent a half-hour in the roar of the rear head howling down the flushing stainless-steel toilet, letting off fear and energy into the shivering wake of the rocketing jetliner.

But in Honolulu the cloud did not go away. A flashbulb exploded and a lei was held out. He felt the brush of brown skin he could not have, and cabs and baggage-checks and hundreds and thousands and millions of people as if the pope and president were arriving together on the next flight.

Benjamin ricocheted to the ticket counter of one of the small local airlines, bought a ticket to the smallest airport they serviced, and waited at the last boarding gate, far out in the Siberia of boarding gates, until a DC-3 chattered to the end of the yellow line outside the windy doorway.

The plane was waiting.

Benjamin sat alone in the small waiting room, his new surfboard waiting at his feet . . . waiting. It was quiet in the room, but through the window he could see the slow-motion reverse shadow of the props and knew they were turning loud outside. But no one came. He heard the announcements for arrivals and departures burst into the room, close and authoritative, alive and demanding. And he waited.

And the announcements came slowly—so slowly into his ears—echoing down long corridors into his brain and banging out notes of meaning that played off-key and off-tune and flew apart like exploding silverware. And the announcements came fast, arrivals and departures at 78 rpm, so that planes were landing and taking off every second and baggage carriers shot around in time-lapse haste and people moved in a high-anxiety stammer until the whole airport was a blur except for the DC-3 waiting, its propellers slow shadows—reversed—of strong, thundering speed.

Benjamin pushed open the glass door. Felt the warm press of the hard tropic wind. Smelled the sea and pineapple and the awful cough of industry. He pushed out against the wind, which seemed suddenly more powerful than any wind before. It pulled hard on his board, threatened to snatch it from him, take it up into itself. Benjamin's pants were pulled skin tight against his legs, his shirt molded over his chest. His cheeks flapped in rippling waves. The wind tore at his lips, burst into his mouth, drove fingers into his eye sockets, and pulled hard on his hair.

Yet the door on the side of the plane swung lazily open, the propeller shadows moving slower now, and always backwards. Through the dark glass of the cockpit Benjamin detected some faint, affirmative motion. He trudged on, angled into the incredible wind until he came close to the open door, where suddenly everything went still. Leaning into the abrupt calm, he nearly fell over. He looked around. The wind had stopped. Nothing moved but the slow-motion propellers. There was no sound as he climbed into the plane. No sound as the door closed. No sound as the plane taxied off.

When the flight steward came for his ticket, Benjamin was amazed at how well the man moved for his age. He appeared to be several hundred years old. He smiled warmly, though, and his eyes were very much alive. He ripped the ticket in half with a sure, fine tear.

"What time is it?" Benjamin asked.

"For you or for me?" the steward said.

I'll just look out the window, Benjamin decided.

But instead, when the steward had gone, he looked around at all the rows and rows of empty seats.

"Hey, man, wake up," the second Malibu surfer said.

"What?" the first one asked.

"Time to grow a little more."

"All right!" the first Malibu said. "Nothin' I dig more 'n a little growth!"

There was a whole new emotion in Benjamin as he sat in the warm sand, watching the first wave of a big, perfect set uncoil, spitting.

There was peace in his soul and clarity in his head.

A surfer named Buck, who had once been Mister Rincon, squatted beside him, a serene, blissful smile on his face as he, too, watched that first wave. Buck had been here almost ten years. He was almost forty and very young.

There were three surfers in the water, far out at the indicator, beyond a point of sand and palms. As one of them turned and stroked into the second wave of the set, Buck raised his arm and pointed. Benjamin grinned into the sun, shielded his eyes with a hand.

He saw the surfer drop straight down, make a clean, slow, powerful turn at the bottom and angle up into the deep central curve of the wave, bringing his trim-line into perfect phase with flow of the wave. He stood there, slightly crouched and relaxed, until the barrel of the wave moved over him. Then he was out of sight.

And yet Benjamin could see him all the more clearly now. Could see his energy alive in the mind of the wave and in his own surge of total empathy and understanding.

"I never knew," Benjamin said.

"None of us did," Buck said.

"Incredible."

Down the beach, the surfer pulled out of the wave with a clean, twisting throw of spray. He pulled back out to the point with neat, sure strokes—effortlessly and incredibly fast—while the third and fourth waves of the set were ridden by the other two surfers.

Benjamin watched and wondered.

"I want to do some words," he said after the fourth wave, watching them paddle back out towards the point.

"I will listen," said Buck.

Once I thought that it was in me. I thought it was a way to some recognizable achievement. I thought that if I could be the best, then I would be able to live with myself.

There were people there in the beginning that I envied and respected. Each of them was like a diamond, a perfect individual, so totally alive and self-sufficient. And I looked at them and then looked at myself and knew that I had to be like them. Except that all I could see was that they were the best. It never occurred to me to ask myself why they were the best. It never crossed my mind that before I could be like them I had to find out what I was.

So I went out there and learned to rip, and in the end all I was doing was laying my trip on the waves. Turning the ocean into an arena for my ego.

And now I know why: I thought that it was in me.

Every time I rode a wave well, I paddled back out thinking what power I had. What strength and energy. How fine and noble a man could be!

But it was the wave.

All that energy coming all those miles to touch bottom over solid, sudden reefs and throw up and out and strain against all the forces until they snap and there's that explosion, and then they're zippering off like a fuse from point to cove. And the surfer sits in that coil of pure juice, and there is definitely a charge there, a holy void full of sprung energy, that permeates the surfer, feeding him all that strength and energy and positive juice. And when he cuts out of the wave feeling strong and alive, if he is stupid enough, he takes credit for the way he feels. He strokes himself with a surge of self-pride and adds more weight to his ego. The wave is dead, and its power has been wasted by the surfer.

The rider of waves must be a humble man; I see that now. To maximize the forces, he must minimize himself. The ego is a dead end. It is an interruption between the outside and the inside. It is a wall. But if he is open and selfless, the surfer will pick up the energy that rebounds around him and store it in the cells of his soul; and that energy will give him the clarity and purity to live an aware life.

The whole world is built on man's biggest mistake: taking credit for what he is allowed to do. It is insecure greed that has made some men greater than others.

The hunger of the ego has covered the world with false power networks that feed on the life force, building walls of illusion around minds that take credit for all that God has done.

Though Buck made no sign of movement, Benjamin knew that he had heard every word, had known every word. They watched another set come. Watched the three surfers sit back, riding in the deep energy.

"I need some information," Benjamin said after the waves had died.

"Yes," Buck said.

This place came quite naturally into being. When the first of us began to see what we all can see, he was brought to this place simply because this is the place where people like us can be. It's one place in the universe where we can live uncompromised and with peace of mind. In time we are all going to be here, simply because this is the only place on the game board that is not hostile to us. Once you lose your ego, the world is no safe place. The greed-filled men will suck up your juice to feed themselves. We have to find places like this. Places that are not on their maps, because their maps are maps of illusion laid over reality. And there are no illusions. And no things. Just every surfer that had the realization that *it* was not in himself.

All the faces that have disappeared from the beaches and the waves, all the people that threaded the network until it was too fine to thread, all the surfers who surrendered to their souls . . . they're all here.

And we'll be right here till everyone who is coming is here, and in the end this place will be reality, and games of power and hate will be fictions of deranged minds, because they are.

Benjamin waited a few feet outside of the reef, watching the boils of air roil up from underwater, watching the patterns of energy escaping to the surface, waiting for the next wave.

A bus roars by . . . policeman raises white-gloved hand and says, "C'mon! C'mon!"

All alone, rocking on the turquoise sea, watching clean clear water slosh between his thighs. Feeling at peace for the first time in a thousand years.

Impact drill goes to work busting concrete sidewalk . . . three yellow cabs jockey for a single old lady with a brown shopping bag . . . a door above flies open and a skinny black kid comes out backwards tumbling head over heels down the brownstone steps and out onto the sidewalk where the old lady is getting into the cab . . . and three bigger, blacker kids come quickstepping down and proceed to beat the skinny kid as the one lucky cab screams away into the night of noon.

And the set rose up out of the deeps, swelling with imminence and purpose, heaving suddenly, surely and inexorably into its full, final destiny. And Benjamin, being there, began to stroke into its rhythm.

But just as they are loosening the white keyboard of his teeth, the National Guard explodes around the corner of 23rd and Main, marching like a single body to the blare of huge unintelligible speakers that demand some immediate action from the populace along the lines of surrender. A color TV in a shop window shows the president having breakfast with a premier in a palace. A young woman stands dark and naked at her washbasin trying to squeeze another brushing from a mangled tube of Crest. And outside there is this Fourth of July crackle . . .

So Benjamin felt the slide that soon became a drive—a thrust—as the tendon of this liquid muscle went taut and flexed a steady line from point to bay. He drove off the bottom and into the deepest part of the gut. He drew a line toward infinity and took a good deep breath.

From the restaurant atop the Bankers' Club, a table-for-six looks out over the city, down on 23rd and Main, and sees the puffs of smoke and hears nothing but Bert Kemphert and "Red Roses for a Blue Lady," and one says, "There go the interest rates again!" and the others laugh and order another round as the TV explodes out across Main to the opposite gutter where four souls have forgotten their differences in death.

Benjamin flew through the charged hold of the wave. He felt the atmosphere grow thick with power and ozone. Sprung energy was everywhere, and he opened himself to receive it. He surrendered to the power of the wave, humbled himself to it, and was rewarded with a full dose of pure life force.

"Aw shit!" the old man snaps, changing the channel. "Same old goddamn crap—riots and starvation and killings and rapes and hippies and people knockin' the president. I ain't gonna watch the news no more!"

"I'm free!" Benjamin rejoiced. "I am free of my old, hung-up self. I am free of everything but life force. I am free of all but the God within me!

A bus roars by . . . p'liceman raises white-gloved hand and says "C'mon! C'mon!" as Benjamin stalls the car, puts it in neutral, turns the key, then puts it in first and starts out across the intersection, passing the cop who looks like someone he's seen before.

How thin the veil of illusion! How fine the line that separates man from the world! How near the inner and the outer! How real the peace of unreality! How unreal the real . . .

But after all, Benjamin thought, it's all a state of mind.

He settled down into the warm sand of the pit. Malibu was four feet. It was late September.

"Right on the tip?" somebody asked.

"Toes over."

"Shit."

He sat in the sun, turning brown in the heat, feeling unsettled and driven and faintly aware that the ocean seemed to be filled with surfers who were never there before.

And then the feeling was gone and lost like a dream, and there was nothing but the white-gloved hand of the cop in the rear-view mirror.

This story originally appeared in the Australian magazine Tracks *in 1974 and has been revised.*

douglas la mancha
and the razor bay rippers

THE MORNING WAS GRAY AND COLD and a south wind crumbled the two-foot surf into a chaos of misery for the teams of young men that periodically took to the water for the event of the day, a minor-league surf contest pitting the Sanderling Pointmen against the Razor Bay Rippers, for whom insult was being added to injury. The Pointmen were up 34 to 8 in the 7th session, and there was literally nothing on the horizon as Morey Sanchez sat on the bench worrying without focus, massaging his numb, aching knees, and wondering what to do.

Was anything humanly possible?

Just two months ago, things had looked promising. The Rippers had launched into the preseason meets with three strong surfers heading the lineup. Then Biltcher got busted for caffeine and tobacco (the fool!) and heavily fined and banned from the league for two years. It was a tragedy for a genuine asshole who could have become good enough to go up to the Majors. Biltcher was just a kid, Morey rationalized, but he was a stupid kid.

Then Ziffle was arrested with Duane Longley, who never had a prayer anyway, but that was it for Barney—guilt by association—what a mess! On his own, Barney Ziffle would never have attempted surfing Rancho Concepcion—the kid was red-hot, but he lacked the violent imagination to surf the Out-of-Bounds. No, Longley had talked him into it, probably claiming he had Platinum Coastal Access. Fat chance. Longley was a duck. Now Ziffle would do a little time, then be paraded before the League Tribunal. He'd have his access downgraded to Local Only status for maybe a year, and there goes his shot at the Bigs. Confined to local waves meant he'd spend a year fighting the crowds at the Generator Peaks near his home in the South Bay, which translated into a year almost certainly without progress. While his peers would be traveling the world surfing a never-ending series of long, hollow AA-Spots, Barney'd be confined to the available blown-out junk.

Of course, he was lucky this wasn't the good old days when the surf in the South Bay was really bad, randomly organized by drifting sand and seasonal runoff. Now, even though the wind was still straight onshore most of the time, at least there were plenty of perfectly organized peaks—a left and a right for every generator reef from Venice to Redondo: sixty-three symmetrical submarine chevrons honeycombed with two-way surge generators and staggered at varying depths to keep the juice flowing to eighteen million Los Angeles consumers. Even so, it was a sorry place to stick a talent like Barney Ziffle.

But worst of all was Dean Stanton. Twelve years in the Majors, then wham! Two big injuries, one right after the other, put him on Injured Disability. After recovering from the first injury, he came to Razor Bay to get back up to speed and led the Minors with a 9.785 average and 5 Golden Barrels, and the Rippers made it to the playoffs, where they lost in a tiebreaker to Malibu. That was four years ago.

But then Stanton hurt himself again, and it was the head, not the ankles, and when he came back through Razor Bay, he just wasn't right. His average was still a respectable 9.6 or so, but there were no Golden Barrels this time, and the Rippers had only an average year. That was the year before last.

Last year Dean was strong and getting stronger. He was so confident he was surfing Nakeds by early winter, and he was snapping at the heels of Turner, Mossburgh, and Snyder, and he would have caught them at Hatteras if Anskeller hadn't taken the opportunity to exercise his Revenge Privilege right then and there. He'd clearly been saving it all year for the occasion, and Morey was both affronted and embarrassed by this incredibly personal gesture, which was the note that ended the year for Razor Bay and Dean Stanton.

So this year they began with God on their side, and they came out firing in the preseason. And that's when Biltcher and Ziffle went down, and Stanton (who wasn't likely to surf for Razor Bay all year anyway, since he was basically back to Majors form) took a fin in the skull from Moss Beach's Masamba Beauchamp and had to be airlifted to the Marin Headlands HoiPaloi Hospital, where he was pronounced Noncontributory and resettled in stasis housing, while being further downgraded with theramones. Morey knew without a doubt that he'd never surf again, with all that implied, and for a guy like Stanton it implied very much indeed, because Dean Stanton was one of the very few surfers in the last twenty years who had a real shot at a dozen Golden Barrels in a single season. And that meant Full Access, and that meant full freedom—no restrictions of any kind, anywhere. It was a dream they all had, but only one out of a million achieved it.

The last surfer to make Full Access was the legendary Foss Benchly, who actually reached the Waterman's Dozen mark—13 Golden Barrels. Foss the Boss was retired to Albatross 14, a synthetic atoll about 300 miles off the tip of Baja, where he not only retired from surfing, he retired from all self-discipline. He became addicted to Pseudew and avocados and finally heart-attacked while lying in the back of his replica '48 Ford woody at age forty-three. He weighed over 525 pounds. His last words, Morey had heard, were "Here comes a big set."

It was a pity, of course, but reminiscing about the Boss's exploded anatomy wasn't going to solve his immediate problem: Was anything humanly possible?

Out in the water, Fairchild and Webster were being eaten alive by Spivey and Everett "Little Boy" Floyd. Spivey had an aerial repertoire that was blindingly complex and sick. The Judgment Board was routinely over thirty seconds behind on his waves as the judges slowed the replay down to a point where they could actually count the endos, rollos, overos, buckminsters, and hiccups. He was a human flurry. And Floyd, while more classically inclined, was no slouch either. His reverse barrel rides were sensational, even in this pathetic junk. They made an excellent Doubles team.

As for his own riders—Dana Webster and Duffy Fairchild—there was nothing much to say. They were competent but utterly uninspiring. They knew some team strategy but had no finesse; everything was obvious. They were the kind of surfers that could put a gallery to sleep or send thousands packing down the beach to the volleyball arena.

Morey stood up, groaned almost silently at the three-pronged pains from his knees and lower back, and slogged through the sand to the fluid caddie. He slipped his mug briefly under the Pseudew spout, then became aware of his sagging gut and thought better of it. He took a double dose of Gin-Sing instead, then turned towards his bench as he sipped the stimulating brew.

He groaned again at the meager range of options and the tight corner into which the fates had forced him. He didn't want his career to end like this, as it most certainly would end if he didn't somehow find a way to win a few meets in a damn hurry. The Rippers were sitting dead last in the league, and this year's last-place coach was by definition next year's migrant laborer, confined to odd jobs in the virtual intelligence ghettos of decaying American suburbs. He shivered at the thought as he scanned the bench: Primakov, Whittacher, Samuals, Dunning, Chang, Bistattler, Woo, McAllister, Gilovich, Lumundu, Mickey Moku, La Mancha . . .

"La Mancha. Has it sunk to this?" he wondered to himself, smirking at the little man on the far end of the bench, his downturned toes just barely wiggling at the sand, that stupid half-smile on his pudgy over-large face, his scraggly tangle of thinning hair already receding past his ears and down his furry little back. Morey's own daughter thought he was cute with his hawklike beak of a nose, and Joe Foxboro in management thought he'd "juice up the team," so there he sat, right where Morey in all his vindictive self-indulgence had let him sit for— what?—over a month now, at the end of the bench.

The repeating bleep signaling the end of the session took Morey's attention back to the business at hand. "What a comedy!" he thought. "My whole life has become like twentieth-century theater of the absurd." Only it wasn't the twentieth century anymore.

"Gilovich!" barked Morey, summoning the gentle giant from the middle of the bench. The big blonde approached.

"Get some waves, will ya, Dane?" whined Morey. "And if y' can't get any waves, don't let them have 'em, huh?" Gilovich shrugged in a way that told Morey the guy'd be back selling used magnecars within the year. "Sheeeze!" he marveled as he watched Big Dane lope over to the board rack and draw out his blade-thin six-footer. Then, on an impulse, without looking back at the bench, he muttered the momentous name for the first time, "La Mancha."

He didn't say it loud. It was a conversational tone, spoken into the face of the onshore wind that drifted back towards the sparsely populated gallery. And yet he almost immediately sensed a presence behind his left elbow.

"Ah!" he said, turning more on a feeling than anything, "La Mancha." Douglas stood there, summoned and ready, small and steady. He was a leash's length shy of six-foot, which put him a tad under four, and he wore one of those old baseball caps with the holographic logo in front. It read "Angels."

"Give it a try, lad. Do what you can."

Morey's glance was too cursory to see the fire his words kindled in La Mancha's beady black eyes; he turned back to the sea to watch Gilovich wade out into the shorebreak, duck under a thick, brown section, and stroke out towards the peaks between the two Sanderling seeds, B. K. Tomey and Carlos Inez. "What difference could it make?" Morey wondered to himself. Tomey and Inez were both very good surfers; in fact, Inez was heading to the Rippers when management, as usual, co-opted his coach's prerogative by bringing in Duffy Fairchild, a mediocre switch foot, who pushed them right up against the salary cap with not a prayer of salvaging the season. Rumor was someone on the Board owed Fairchild's father a favor.

"Ay-yee," sighed Morey, idly massaging an aching shoulder as he watched the dwarf La Mancha in neolithic baggies following the three big surfers out into the butt-ugly shorebreak. As Douglas began his series of duck-dives out to the peaks, Morey surveyed the Saturday morning panorama, from the decrepit mile-long condominium hives to the various crumbling and graffitied community domes and the cracked and overgrown old roads that once chopped the city into "blocks." It was as ugly a sight as the surf, mused Morey. No relief in sight.

He was drifting to that far land of the imagination, where warm barrels spin and goddesses trickle sweet passion-fruit juice into your smiling mouth as you loiter with them on dappled cobalt-blue seas between sets, when a sudden and rare outburst from the bench brought him back to the gray shores of reality.

"Bingo!" shouted Woo.

"Chilly cubed, uncle!" agreed Chang.

Morey looked out and saw Gilovich planing under a crumbling section while Inez and Tomey scratched for the next couple of peaks. He couldn't spot La Mancha.

"What? What?" he demanded, looking back at the boys on the bench.

"The little guy," answered Woo. "What's his name. The midget."

"What?" repeated Morey, looking back out. "Where's he?"

"Down there," said Mickey Moku, pointing. "There!" he repeated when Morey still couldn't find him. Morey turned, caught the direction everyone on the bench was now pointing, and spotted La Mancha's tiny form windmilling back up towards the designated takeoff area. He was moving through the water about as fast as a man could run, and he now had Morey's full attention.

"Sheeeeze," muttered Morey.

By the time the two Sanderling surfers got their peaks and were whittling them to pieces, La Mancha was back in position, paddling into an average peak. And then it was like a revelation out of myth—from the days of Gerry Lopez summoning the peaks of Banzai Pipeline and commanding the door stay open, no matter how absurd the length of the tube, and the people were too asleep to notice the divine incarnate. It was like that.

La Mancha dropped, and his little leaf of a board—about four feet long and two feet wide and shaped like the leaf of an aspen, its nose kicked elegantly, the tail a living plane of energy, looking for all the world like translucent jade—that board arced beneath him in a movement so beautifully fluid yet so utterly fast that it was only an echo and the rider was gone . . . there! . . . banking off the ramp of the next section, redirecting like . . . there is no word for it. Say "like a magician," and you would be close.

Morey reflexively bent over at the waist and squeezed his legs just above the knees. "Sheeeeeeeeeeeze!"

As he watched La Mancha ricocheting down the beach, the clouds above parted and a stab of sunlight glanced off Morey's titanium helmet. Up through the hole in the blue sky, traffic was heavy. It was late Thursday morning, and people were heading out for the weekend.

Things took a turn for Morey then, as they did for the entire Razor Bay Rippers organization. The upside was they were winning every event. The downside was that the Majors were very interested in Douglas La Mancha, and Morey knew fully that the chances of keeping the Mighty Midget a day past the end of the AA Championships was a perfect number: zero.

In fact, the only reason that La Mancha hadn't been moved up to the J-Baysters was that he wouldn't talk to management. He'd listen, but he wouldn't talk, except to say, "No comment," after every pitch.

His contract was one year. Management could either fire La Mancha for his unwillingness to negotiate, sue him for violating the Corporate Protection Act, or let him surf his year in the minors, then bar him from all but Major League Surfing worldwide. They decided to wait and watch. Morey had a championship to win.

Then came the Rule Change: Effective immediately, only maneuvers initiated within the core competition area would be scored. For all of Major League Surfing history, the rule had been that any ride initiated before the expiration of time will be scored till the rider stops riding. Now there would be no wave changes, and no maneuver changes either.

The new rule clearly targeted Douglas, who was famous for making so much angular progress (made both on the face and spinning or gliding through the air) that some of his waves lasted as long as three minutes. If everyone was confined to, say 10 to 15 seconds, there was a much greater chance that La Mancha could be beaten.

It turned out to be a nonfactor. Surfing his first wave of the first heat after the Rule Change (in Niijima vs. Club Best Ever), Douglas ducked into a tube and disappeared. Didn't come out, didn't come up.

The Surfrider E-Boat was heading into the peaks when a cheer went up— La Mancha had cut out of a close-out wave a half-mile down the beach and was seen paddling back up the beach like a buzz saw. The judges were thrown into confusion. It was over a minute before they awarded their score: 0—because they didn't see what happened. It was the equivalent of a DSQ in nanosailing. And even that didn't matter, because Douglas just did it again, and again, and again—somehow he almost always made the longest reverse tubes, the most penetrating spiral moves, the fastest aerial chicanery. Almost every ride a 10. Almost. After all, no matter what people said, Douglas was as human as anyone. His rare wipeouts made for great theater and gave hope to his competitors. Still, he set a mark that no one else will ever match—96 Golden Barrels in a single season . . . and just a six-month season at that!

Then came the Sponsorship Deal: La Mancha signed with one of the world's oldest and largest corporations, McDonald's. The deal was "the news." In acquiring the surfer for the term of his existing contract, the corporation also bought the right to sponsor the surfer, Douglas La Mancha, for the life of his professional surfing career. He was well worth it, McDonald's president William Jefferson Clinton II enthused. After all, an estimated 2.4 billion human beings now watched every Razor Bay competition; it was the most exciting thing on in those days.

In return for his Full Endorsement, La Mancha received $1 million per year (the average salary a Surfrider Caretaker received for patrolling, guarding, and helping to preserve the coastal ecology). However, along with the cash, he won certain concessions from McDonald's. Effective within 30 days, the world's largest restaurant network—with over 100,000 locations and a dozen subsidiary chains, including Amazon Rainforest (genetically-engineered cheeseburgers), Yeltsin Gdansk (old-style taverns with a Y2K Russian Mafia theme), and Mark and Corky's Houses of Pancakes—would convert to a completely organic, cruelty-free, meatless menu offering optimum nutrition to the children of the world (and their elders) at a cost affordable by anyone. Additionally, all restaurants would be redesigned with regenerative building materials (and food-service supplies) for maximum comfort and invisibility; succulent aromas should and would do the advertising. Final condition: Ronald McDonald and his stupid plastic playgrounds would be recycled—no distractions. With his hands on the table and fingers certifiably uncrossed, Clinton personally agreed to keep these changes in place for three years. If, after that time, the corporation wished to return to its earlier practices, it could.*

The extraordinary enforcement powers that went along with the agreement were testament to Douglas La Mancha's world stature, achieved in sudden fashion through the unlikely medium of Minor League Surfing. He had more fans than the previous great legends (Jordan, Spencer, Slater, Lewison, Foss the Boss, Woods, and Kinimaka) combined. These fans wore huge baggies and old-fashioned baseball caps—like their grandparents did in the Gay '90s, except the hologram always read "Angels"—and they talked like DLM talked, referring to the future with an end-over gesture of the hand and the word "yes." Their hair was never combed or brushed, and their philosophy of life was "bingo"—everything's possible in the Yes State. Simple stuff but all bullshit as far as Morey knew. He had no clue as to what made Douglas tick, he just wanted to know how much time was on the clock.

Championships, but Morey still didn't know what to expect. Simply winning the AA World Title would ensure his virtual comfort in some sweet neck of the woods, but it didn't necessarily do much for his career as a coach. Everyone knew why they were winning.

"Y'know Douglas," he said. They were sitting side by side on the bench watching a newly inspired Duffy Fairchild and a sluggish Nikita Primakov (motivated but not very talented) double up on two of Montauk's top guns. "I could exercise my Revenge Privilege and keep you out of the water."

"What?" said Douglas, watching the action while running a Polargizer along the rails of his 48-ounce board.

"This is it—you've got your SemiFinal, then the Final, and then what?"

"What?" Douglas repeated.

"This is it—the SemiFinal, then the Final. After that . . . "

"Before that. What did you say before that?"

"Huh?" Morey looked away, rubbed a knee though it hadn't been hurting.

"Before that—a privilege?"

"Oh that," Morey said, twisting his face apologetically. "I was just joking. Being funny. I . . . it's just that I could, y'know, invoke my Revenge Privilege and keep you out of the water. It was a joke. I was curious. I wanted to ask you what you were going to do, which, I suppose, is sort of connected to what I'm going to do, in a way, depending, but then I said that about the Revenge Privilege. I don't know why, except, I don't know, maybe I'd make a decent coach in the Majors if you were going that way and I was available, which I am of course . . . "

Douglas just looked back at him and said, "No comment."

Then the repeating bleep was signaling the end of the session and La Mancha carefully put down the Polargizer and took off his cap. Morey watched him paddle out with a mixture of suppressed panic and painful regret, which was quickly rewarded when Douglas dropped into a 5-foot wave, fanned a 100-foot-high arc of spray, and disappeared into a pitching tube, backdoor. Down the beach, they waited for him to emerge, but he never did. The E-Boat scoured the place—no trace. That was the end of Douglas La Mancha . . . and Morey Sanchez . . . and the Razor Bay Rippers for that matter.

La Mancha never even made it to the final, which was surfed by Duffy Fairchild—Morey's last stab at tactical appeasement. But Fairchild was humiliated by Lance Hamilton. Within a year the franchise was history as public interest and management patience waned. The disappearance of Douglas La Mancha assumed the same sort of cachet as the disappearance of the twentieth-century aviatrix, Amelia Earhart, except that DLM's bones were never found.

As for Morey, he ended up coaching single-A Surfing in Fort Lauderdale, where over 1,000 new generator reefs—those beautiful symmetrical submarine chevrons—had transformed the coast into a small-wave surfing paradise. The Lauderdale Watersnails were a sorry lot—old pros mostly—including the once-great Barney Ziffle, who was attempting a comeback while continually threatening to flee to Rancho Concepcion and live out his years surfing the Out-of-Bounds.

Whenever someone from the press would ask Morey about Douglas La Mancha, he'd just turn away with a brusque, "No comment." He had learned to hold his tongue, wondering what had possessed him. As he often confided to a good-lookin' waitress at a Lauderdale McDonald's Organica, "Why didn't I wait to talk to him after the final heat?" It was a question that would haunt him until the day he died. That and the last ride of Douglas La Mancha.

ENDNOTE
* As we all know, the Four La Mancha Principles—sloganeered as "full work, full play, square deal, square meal"—are the cornerstones of most corporations today.

This story first appeared in the Winter 2000 issue of The Surfer's Journal.

snaking steve

THERE WERE TWO HOURS TO GO till noon and the black asphalt of the Coast Highway already bubbled under the intense July sun. So when Scott crossed over to the beach, he walked the cool, white line of the crosswalk, his foam board tucked under his left arm, his daypack on his back, and his fins in his right hand. His eyes felt free to wander in the private shadows behind his mirrored sunglasses.

He moved with a growing flood of people that swept in from the bus stops and parking lots and neighborhoods, converging on the foot of the pier where the restaurants, snack shops, bait shops, tourist shops, and—yes—surf shops created a sort of summer-long seaside festival.

Up on the pier, amidst the rumbling hooves of the weekend walkers, Scott could get a good perspective on the surf and on the beach below. He was already plenty hot—the day was as sultry as the night had been—and there was a clammy humidity on his skin despite the heat. That was because of the thundering swell that was pounding the sandbars, shaking the timbers and pilings of the old pier, and misting the hot day with the smoke of a thousand liquid explosions.

The lifeguards will be put to the test today, Scott thought. And then he realized that he, too, might be put to the test.

Above the lifeguard headquarters on the pier, the yellow flag hung straight down in the glaring heat. Below, on the beach, shimmering human fillets—slick with lotions and oils—were roasting on their towels. Scott noticed that more girls were going topless this year, and the bottoms were almost a match.

As he walked further out onto the pier, his bare feet warming to the point of pain even on the bleached planks, he stopped every so often to stand in the shade of the railing and scan the sand below for his friends. Maybe they were in the water already, but probably not—the black-ball flag wasn't up yet for the surfers, even though it was past ten.

There were only a few surfers out, widely scattered by a strong swell pushing up the beach from the south; the period between waves was long—over 15
seconds. The swell was from the southern hemisphere; these waves had come
over seven thousand miles. The shorebreak was a solid four feet, but farther outside huge peaks periodically wedged up, darkened, and pitched over with loud
cracks in the windless summer air. He saw two surfers drop in together, stand,
and get pitched into a frightening dual wipeout. He looked back towards the lifeguard tower almost instinctively and saw that the black ball had been raised.

As he looked back to the water, his vision was flared and spotted from the
sun that stood squarely behind the flags. He noticed a small butterfly racing in
his chest as he neared the end of the pier. Out there, in a world of fishermen
and their tackle, where strolling couples and joggers made their far turns, there
were the open-ocean swells, silently sweeping in, hissing through the outermost
pilings, then crashing over, sending deep seismic shudders the length of the
great spine of the pier. It was easy to feel the power.

Briefly, Scott contemplated saving himself the paddle and jumping off the
pier right into the lineup. They did that sometimes on the bigger swells during
the week. But it was a circus on weekends, and the lifeguards were usually dialed
into their hard-nosed mode, so it probably wasn't worth the hassle. Besides, he
had his daypack.

Walking quickly now, back towards the beach, the public address was order-
ing the last few surfers out of the water. Way inside he could already see the
swing shift starting to go to work—bodyboarders kicking out through the shorebreak. He saw as one guy was pitched mercilessly into a contorted backflip, then
swallowed in a nasty blast of whitewater.

Past the tower he started scanning the southside beach again . . . close up to
the pier where they usually gathered, and finally he saw them—the circle of
friends and their pile of boards, leashes, fins, packs, towels, and clothes . . .
because the clothes were off and the suits were on, and Ozzie was already rubbing a soft wad of wax over the red deck of his board.

Scott stopped directly above them, leaning over the railing, looking down,
the sun hot on his head; his back, under his pack, was soaked with sweat. He
thought he could smell bubble gum.

Below, sitting in the hot sand next to Ozzie, Carlos was playing with one of
his fins. His hair was dark, tangled, and glistening. Carlos and Ozzie were a

pair—the one so compact, solid, and shy; the other, Ozzie, so long and lean and talkative. Ozzie was always analyzing the situation—an endless rap accompanied by his giddy hyena laugh. And Carlos, he'd just snort like a bull and look down at his feet.

Jenny was there too, and Daria. He liked looking at Jenny—he was looking at her now, studying her from behind his sunglasses as she pulled a shorty wetsuit up over her bikini. He liked her positive athletic energy, and her softness too. And Daria . . . he liked her too—her total directness and honesty—though she was by no means as great to look at as Jenny.

While Scott watched from above, Duane joined the other four. He was actually carrying his plastic silver briefcase with him today, plus his small cooler, and his pack, and his board and fins. Duane got a new haircut in June, the day after school was out, so it'd had a month to grow, so he wasn't entirely bald anymore—just sort of dirty looking.

He could hear Ozzie running off at the mouth with Duane, and then Duane popped open his briefcase, took Carlos's fin and started to tinker with the strap. That's when Steve came into the picture, throwing his board with a careless toss that flung sand into the briefcase and onto Daria's legs.

Even on the pier, with all the tramping and blabbing noise of the crowd around him, Scott could hear the hard, sarcastic cadence of Steve's voice. Here was someone Scott didn't even want to know about, but somehow Steve Baily had become an integral part of his summer life. Each and every day this irritating, bullying idiot insinuated himself into their lives. Scott wasn't sure why, except that he was obviously trying to hit on Jenny.

Jenny had been a year ahead of Scott at school, though she was only three months older (she was still seventeen) but she'd graduated in June and was heading off to college. A lost cause, Scott thought, while hoping she wasn't.

Steve was a year out of high school. In fact, Scott remembered his relief last September when there was no longer a chance of seeing him in the hallways between classes. Steve had worked at the surf shop across from the pier for a few months during the winter, and even though he'd been fired before summer, that's where he got his nickname—Snake.

The name fit him perfectly, Scott thought, as he walked off the pier and started down the stairs to the beach. Steve was a snake in every sense of the word—in the water, with money, getting rides, picking on the younger kids, taking advantage of people, and especially with girls.

He wasn't that big—just an inch or two taller and ten pounds or so heavier than Scott—but he was mean. He had a mean mouth and mean eyes that were small and close together. Scott had seen him in a fight in the water back during Easter week, and it hadn't been a pretty thing to watch. He'd wanted to interfere, but he didn't see it start, didn't know what had caused it, so he'd let it go. Afterwards the story was that Steve had snaked the other kid on a set wave, but that the other kid had dropped in anyway. Snake.

It was cool and damp in the shade under the pier. A lot of people had already set up camp there for the day. Scott wove a path through them, heading closer to the roiling power of the waves that blasted the pilings a hundred yards or so ahead, filling the wooden space with sound and energy. Like an atomic cave, Scott thought, as he breathed in the creosote.

Stepping out into the heat and light—bright even through his sunglasses—Scott joined the others. Carlos, his board beside him on the sand, was stretching, his hands clasped above his head, rotating at the waist. He twisted Scott's direction and said, "Hi."

"Hey, Scott," said Ozzie. "Were you a party animal last night or what?"

"Or what," Scott answered.

"Hi, Scott," said Daria. She was lying back on a pure white towel that enveloped her dark brown body in light.

"Hi," said Jenny. Scott looked over, smiled at her, then turned back to Ozzie and Carlos. Steve, sitting next to Jenny, grinned back at Scott.

"Hello, Scott," said Duane. He was rubbing SPF-21 cream all over his wiry neck and shoulders.

"You heading out?" Scott asked, speaking to no one in particular.

"Gonna try to," said Carlos. He stood up, and then the three of them—Carlos, Ozzie, and Scott—stood shoulder-to-shoulder in the heat, looking out over the frying tourists and beached suburbanites at the surf. The water was clear of stand-up surfers now, and only a few bodyboarders and bodysurfers bobbed near the big waves outside.

They watched for a while, trying to pick up the rhythm of the sets. There was a steady, mean six-foot ground swell with good eight-foot sets. But once while they watched there was a single rogue wave that reared up way outside and collapsed with such a loud crack that they could hear it over the ever-present roar of the shorebreak. That one made them swallow hard and look at each other.

"Let's hit it!" came the enthusiastic challenge, but it was from Jenny, starting past them with her board and fins.

"You hit it," Daria called after her. "I'm not ready to die."

While the rest of them quickly gathered up their gear, Scott ran up to Jenny and walked beside her down to the water. "Maybe you should let us try it for a while first," he suggested.

"You're cute," she answered without a smile. "I'm not sitting there for one more second with that jerk." Scott stopped; Jenny splashed into the water, turned and worked her fins on, then flopped onto her board and started kicking out, ducking through the first surge of foam, coming out the back with her hair transformed, swept back in a dark flow of movement. Then Ozzie and Carlos were standing beside him.

"Should she be going out there?" Carlos asked. "Snake," Scott said by way of explanation, jerking his head slightly back towards where Steve was leaning over talking to Daria. Duane was sitting there, too, with a sort of blank expression, holding a screwdriver in his hand like a weapon. And then, for an instant, there was a electric flash of understanding between the three of them—Ozzie, Carlos, and Scott—standing there with the water curling and pulling at their ankles—a momentary communication—and then they turned at the same instant and went back up the beach.

"Ready, men?" asked Ozzie, looking from Duane to Steve to Daria. "Huh? Huh? Huh?"

"Yeah," said Duane, dropping the screwdriver into his case, then snapping it shut. "You watch this for me?" he asked Daria.

"It's a man's world out there," Ozzie said to Steve. "You up to it?"

Steve turned, sneered vaguely, lethargically, then stood up and looked around like a bear coming out of hibernation. Then he looked squarely at Ozzie. "Don't talk to me, okay? I get sick to my stomach."

They started paddling out together, the five of them, but the first set split them up. The water was surprisingly cool for such a hot day. That sometimes happened on a south swell, Scott recalled. He was caught inside on a set, and it took him a while to find Jenny. When he did, Steve was there in the water beside her.

They were out pretty far, and big peaks wedged in, looking like they'd break, lifting them and moving on inside. Ozzie, Carlos, and Duane broke over the top of one, just making it through. Steve was trying to get Jenny to go to the Ratt concert with him. Jenny was trying to get Steve to vanish from the face of the earth. Scott was trying to figure out a way . . .

"Leave her alone, Steve." It was Ozzie.

"Shut up," Steve said with a quick hard glance and nothing more. He turned back to Jenny, who was kicking away—further out and closer to the pier. He started to paddle after her.

"Leave her alone." This time it was Duane. Steve stopped, spun to face him, paddled back a ways to confront the four of them.

"Who says?" he challenged. "Shut your faces or I'll shut 'em for you. I got no time for this."

"Neither does Jenny," said Carlos. "She don't want to talk to you."

"Come 'ere," said Steve, emphasizing it with a finger.

"You come here," said Ozzie who was now right beside Carlos. Duane moved over to join them. Scott floated off to the side; he could see Jenny sitting near the pier now, watching them. Steve's back was to her as she pointed outside. Scott looked out, knowing before he saw it what was coming, controlling his own urge to scramble for safety.

"I'll drown you rats one at a time," Steve was saying. His face was red and pinched up like a mad dog's. Scott caught the attention of the others, motioning with his eyes to the huge, steepening wedge. Ozzie went bug-eyed for a split second, then shut it off before Steve caught on—because Steve's back was turned to the horizon and the approaching wave.

Scott was making those internal calculations a bodyboarder learns to make—subtle measurements of the forces at play in an attempt to evaluate the tolerances in a particular situation, which, in this case, was growing critical.

Steve was oblivious to everything but his rage. The four others fanned out in front of him, for the first time ever offering a solid resistance. But, really, they were just an audience in the front row, watching this small, irate little jerk— imagining he was going to snuff them each out, one by one—about to be annihilated by the most massive wave that any of them had ever had the pleasure of sharing the water with.

In fact, as the huge wall of water lifted high into the sky before them— dwarfing Steve at the foot of its ominous vertical presence, Scott felt a most serene satisfaction. He even had a moment to glance out at Jenny. That's when his mouth fell open. She was kicking into the wave!

Framed against the backdrop of the barnacle-encrusted pilings, she was the picture of a fragile creature caught in the grim clutches of the beast. She teetered a second or two in the fringing lip, then started to race down the face, leaping the ledging moguls as she dropped into the awesome pit.

Steve's eyes followed Scott's. You could read the sequence of perceptions in his changes of expression—seeing Jenny skydiving down this giant wave—a brief flash of envy and competition followed by a quick shadow of confusion and a darkening awareness, then a panicked turn of his head to face the awful monster at the worst possible moment.

In that moment, Scott, Carlos, Ozzie, and Duane had made their moves. A few quick strokes and they were past Steve, burrowing deep into the maw of the wave, tunneling up through its huge, heaving back towards the sky.

They broke up through the backside into the hissing aftermath. The deep, resonant rumble of the wave moved towards the beach like a fading freight train, and the briny hiss and smell of shaken ocean was in the air. Scott anxiously surveyed the foaming panorama, but there was no sign of Jenny . . . or Steve . . . until someone blasted over the top of the wave way inside and began kicking back out.

Scott strained his eyes to see who it was, but he couldn't yet. He looked up at the white glare of the sun . . . he'd forgotten it was there, and how, already, it was drying his shoulders and making his eyes itch. He looked over at the pier, at the hundreds of people looking down at the waves and at them. In the calm of the lull and the still air he could hear their voices. But he still couldn't see who it was kicking out towards them.

"It's Steve, and he's gonna suck the eyes out of your head," said Ozzie.

"Nah, it's that ghoul that works at the gas station that stole your fins last summer," said Duane.

"Well, for sure it ain't Jenny," said Carlos.

"It's Jenny," said Scott, though he wasn't absolutely sure yet, but then Ozzie let out his stoked hyena laugh—it echoed in the tunnel of the pier and bounced back at them off the beach and danced around them as they sat on the surface of the sea gone flat.

Scott squinted at the sponger kicking towards them, saw the white flash of a smile, felt the comfort and the camaraderie of his friends, and knew that the summer wasn't such a lost cause after all.

This story first appeared in a 1987 edition of Bodyboarder *magazine.*

sixty6

AUGUST 1966, A HOT NIGHT in the San Fernando Valley near Los Angeles. I was staying with a friend and his wife in an apartment in Reseda, and I was suffocating. Despite the perennial drought, the air outside was damp. Vapors hung over the city, rising from pools and sprinklers, mating with all the other sweet and acrid particulates, creating a uniquely L.A. atmospheric brew. But the screen on the window might as well have been a wall; no air passed in or out. It was dead still.

On an impulse, I snapped up out of bed, straightened the blankets, threw the wet pillow on a chair, and folded the hide-a-bed back into the sofa. I replaced the cushions, grabbed the pillow and the rest of my things, wrote a short note—"Gone surfing. Back late."—and slipped out, locking the door behind me. Down the concrete steps, around the oily slick pool with its sheen of reflected lights, through the iron gate with a clack and a click, and out to the street, where my tan 1960 VW Westphalia van was parked beneath the light at the end of the cul-de-sac between two more ordinary cars. (The long apocalyptic surf poem grease-penned on the side of my van definitely set it apart.)

Outside, the night was warm but with the clammy chill so common in Southern California. The vinyl seat was cold on the underside of my legs where my shorts didn't cover them. I found the ignition slot on the column. The engine jogged a few steps, then fluttered off into an idle. I jockeyed back and forth a few times to get purchase, then swung out from the curb and down the street. I was headed southwest across the valley towards the Ventura Freeway, cool wind laced with warm puffs coming in through the pulled-back half windows, the dash lights dim and faintly yellow, the way they are in old six-volt electrical systems, the headlights on the road ahead scarcely brighter.

In two or three miles I came to the freeway, took the first on-ramp, and labored up the grade (and like any decent owner of a 36 hp VW, I always labored when my van labored). West I rolled, the freeway almost empty at just after 3:00 a.m. Winding out through the west end of the valley, past Calabasas, I took the Las Virgines Canyon turnoff and—the road now completely deserted—chugged south towards the coast. A dim half moon was sinking in sick greens behind the smooth black silhouettes of the mountains to the west, and the night was so dark now that the beams from my headlights seemed satisfyingly bright as I danced through the familiar easy curves, straightaways, and tight S-turns—driving through occasional bubbles of very cool air deep in the tangy canyon vaults— until I took the last sharp right-hand curve and saw the lights along the Pacific Coast Highway far below.

I turned left at the highway (no one was coming) and puttered slowly south a half-mile or so, pulling alongside a row of parked cars at Surfrider Beach, just north of the Malibu pier. I was surprised to see so many cars, but I found a spot and backed in tight to the curb, turned off the ignition, and listened to the surge and sigh of the ocean replace the staggering shutdown of the little four-cylinder engine. The air here was still, too, but it was so heavy with sage and salt that it pressed into the van and filled me with lush and powerful sensations.

After a minute, I got out, took a leak into the bushes over near the famous graf-fitied Malibu wall, then went back to the van and opened out the side doors. I shoved my surfboard over and propped the nose up on the driver's-side seat, then slipped in under it onto the bed to get some sleep before dawn, leaving the doors open to collect the sound and smell of the coast. But I couldn't sleep or even really rest. That sound, and the smell, and knowing I had no alarm to wake me up . . .

I climbed out again at about 4:30, took off my shirt, and locked up the front of the car. Then I went around to the back and opened it up and drew out my 9-foot 6-inch Con surfboard and a quarter bar of Parawax. Then I slammed and locked the rear hatch, hid the keys off a corner of dusty metal up underneath the driver's side front wheel well, and picked my way carefully, barefoot, along the soft roadside dust and glass to the sandy notch that led down the small slope and around the end of the wall and out onto the beach.

There was enough light from the Malibu Inn and the pier that I could see a little of the beach. Sure enough, there were some couples here and there, lying on blankets or just on the sand. I could hear a steady roll of surf and dim curtains of whitewater drawing shoreward out of the dark, invisible ocean. I walked a hundred yards or so up the beach, away from the lights, then laid my board on the sand, waxed it, slipped the wax into the inside pocket of my trunks, and walked down to the water.

The air was cooler down here, and the first touch of wet sand under my feet was cold and I was covered with goose bumps and shivers, but then a foamy sheet of water washed over my feet and around my ankles and it was Southern California summertime warm. I guided the board carefully in the dark as my feet pawed tentatively over the barnacled cobble and occasional larger chunks of slippery rock. When the water was at my crotch, I threw the board up onto a whitewater surge and slid stomach-first onto the waxed deck and paddled hard out into the darkness. I bashed through a couple of whitewater surges, then punched through the face of a dim black wall that was on the verge of breaking, and then I was out the back and clear of the sets.

It was a momentous day. I was going to ride the first wave at Malibu on a south-swell August morning. Something not so easy to do anymore in 1966, when there were often a hundred or more surfers packing the lineups on a warm, classy day. Sometimes a perfect small summer wave wrapping into Malibu would become so crowded with surfers as it broke, it seemed to slow and sag under the burden. And out in the lineup it was a cross-section of the sport's hierarchy. Especially this summer, with the World Contest coming up in October in San Diego. Today was going to be very crowded, but at least I'd have a few rare waves to myself . . . soon.

I could almost see the swells sweeping towards me now out of the blue-black southwest. It was hard to tell, but they seemed three or four feet high, a perfect size for fun and snappy little waves that go curling into the small bay at Surfrider.

From the water, looking back towards the pier, the reflected lights revealed the pulses of swell as they rushed towards the beach. I could see the line of a wave as it passed steeply underneath me, lifting me high, stretching and wrapping south towards the pier, and I studied the viscosity of the water surface as it was stretched and ripped by the curling muscles of wave further towards shore.

How soon, I wondered, would it be light enough to see? To see that wave coming and turn and ride it, the first wave of the day at Malibu. Despite the sweet and bitter aroma and cool breeze that drifted out across the water to me every couple of minutes, I was drifting into a reverie when I found myself listening to voices. Two guys talking quietly, unintelligibly, just above a whisper. With a start and a sudden feeling of panic, I realized there were two other surfers out there in the water with me. Maybe three? Drawn by the voices, I could see their forms now, pale and dark against the black, dimly revealed by the lights on the pier.

I was suddenly embarrassed, awkward. I sucked in my gut, made purposeful paddling gestures as I sat upright on my board. Ashore, the high, crisp line of the Santa Monica mountains was clearly defined now in bright deep blue. Out towards the point I could now discern a string of surfers—ten, twenty—I couldn't tell except that I was not alone. In fact, I appeared to be the surfer furthest south around the point towards the pier. In a world of territory and positioning (and surfing is such a world), if I stayed where I was, I was low man on the totem pole. I'd have to defer to anyone riding a wave this way from the point, since the wave broke from far out that way and peeled towards the spot where I was sitting. First guy to drop in on a wave has possession. Anyone else is dropping in, barging, cutting off, leeching, and looking for trouble. But out there at the tip of the point, it was going to be the usual pack, and that was no fun either, unless you were one of the core boys.

Luckily, I was used to this scenario. Avoiding the pack out at the point, I generally played the game of trying to pull other "inside" guys in too far towards the beach or out too far into the cove. I knew that on most waves there was a large section that curled over just up the point from where I was sitting, and on some waves it was too fast for any but the best surfers to cross to the inside where I waited. I would line up the wave, paddle for it, and wait on the far side of this section to see if the surfer with possession was going to make it. When it became clear he wasn't, or if he fell, I paddled into the wave and often had the last, sometimes excellently shaped, section of wall to myself, right down into the cove, sometimes right to the pier.

So I decided to wait where I was, since now the softening dawn was showing me a dark burnished purple Pacific with a pinkening dark sky and a flotilla of dark silhouettes, other guys like me who'd paddled out in the dead of night to wait here for the first wave.

And then, suddenly, someone else has it—somebody with better night vision than I. He goes slipping by, shooting past like a swift bird between me and the beach, although I hear nothing but the snap and the surging roar of the wave that has just passed beneath me, until (a few seconds later) a small, private whoop pierces the cascade of the inside shorebreak.

Other surfers follow as the morning comes on, dark shapes, crouching or flailing or posing even in this dim light. Yet it's another fifteen minutes before my own eyes get enough depth perception to anticipate and line up with the approaching swells, and then I have to watch that big section to the left, hoping someone will fail to make it through so I can drop in and ride one. But they keep making it through. One after another after another—the section is holding up just long enough for them to skate under the lip and ahead of the curl and into the area of the wave where I'm waiting. I paddle for wave after wave, pushing forward into the rushing whoosh of spray in the suspended lip, only to pull back as a committed rider streaks by.

The sharp ridge of the mountains is brilliant yellow-gold now, fading through green up to powder blue and then into a darker, deeper blue. The western horizon is pink and silver with cloud and reflected dawn. The sun is just about ready to rise and stab my eyes when I spot a band of dark water approaching from out beyond the point, followed by another, and another. It's a good set, the biggest by far this morning. I wheel my board around, lay down on my belly, and paddle like hell straight out towards the building walls.

Despite the jitterbugs twisting in my stomach, I grow exultant with each deep stroke of hands and arms into the water. The first wall of water is the most incredible impression! I surge across a surface of glistening deep purple ripples, smooth as a lake and textured by the morning wind out of Malibu Canyon. Lying prone and paddling, I can't be sure how big it is until I see someone drop in out at the point. It's about three feet over his head and torquing into a clamshell concave when he jams a bottom turn and starts flying down the line in my direction.

The wave is walled straight across from the point to the pier and zippering off perfectly, with one of Malibu's best surfers poised perfectly in the cup of the curl (I can't remember who, maybe it was Cowboy Henderson), and I'm paddling so hard going up the face, watching the perfect symmetry of surfer and curl as I work, that I go airborne for a few feet off the top and splash down hard beyond. The next wave is darker and bigger and already fringing, and Lance Carson is carving and banking and trimming so perfectly that he laces the wave together in one long, perfect ride. No chance for me to turn and take it anyway; it's too hollow already when I claw up the face and over.

The third wave is a little bigger still and just as perfect. Now I'm in the right spot to turn and paddle into it, but three guys are already on it, chasing down the point towards me, carving arcs around the litter of boards and swimmers caught inside by the big set.

Knowing three waves to a set is about all you can expect at Malibu, I paddle up and over the wave feeling like I've missed another opportunity, as the three dance past behind me.

But there is a fourth, as big and perfect as the third, and there's nobody left to ride it! I paddle out to meet it, breathing hard and concentrating because now I fear more than anything the possibility of wasting something so absolutely pristine, this gift of the perfect wave and the perfect moment.

I spin towards shore just ahead of the advancing wall, dig deep in a crawling series of paddles, and pull myself down the face of the wave. I jump to my feet, trim straight down to the hollowing bottom of the wall, then lean into a big, carving turn towards the shoulder, seeing the long, sweet wall extend ahead of me all the way to the pier just as the beam of the sun clears the ridge and sends a hot flash into my eyes.

Blinking away the spots, gathering speed, my board chattering across an impeccable wall of dark water gilded with sunlight, the warm sage-scented wind rushing at my face, I can't begin to imagine a finer moment. I've caught the first wave of the day at Malibu, it's 1966, and I'm stoked. Totally stoked. You would be, too.

This story first appeared in the June 2000 edition of LongBoard *magazine.*

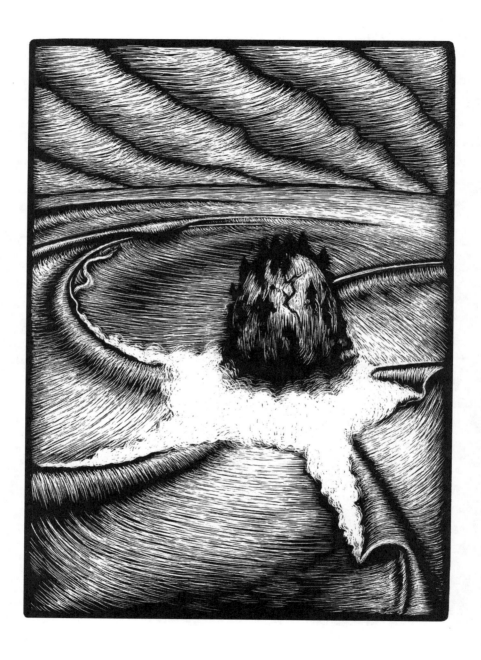

a long-ago tale
of the unending wave

Once, long ago, the World was much smaller. Either that or it was much larger, though it actually doesn't matter which. Then, too, there was Land and Sea, Mountain and Lake, Village and City, Sun and Moon; but on a different scale. There were the Farmers and the Merchants, the Families and the Vagabonds, the Builders and the Destroyers, the Soldiers and the Sailors, the Rich and the Poor. And between it all were the bands of irrepressible rascals who rode the Waves: the nomadic tribes of Surfers.

These coastal nomads led quite a strange existence. While politics and war and the struggle for wealth occupied the people who lived in the beehive cities, these Wave Riders scavenged and frolicked their lives away, paying no heed whatsoever to the laws of the civilized world.

And how they managed to live and thrive, the citizens of the civilized world did not, and could not, understand. This is a little tale about those times.

FROG HUSHED HIS CROAK AND squatted back in the trees. Surfers were coming along the winding road. He could hear their songs and laughter and an occasional rough exclamation. He waited and watched, then saw them burst around the final bend and into the patch of sunlight and the clearing.

They were a bronzed and hearty trio, two with streaming blonde hair and white eyes, one with kinky blonde hair and bright, bright blue eyes. They were speaking in the language of water, so Frog could understand them. And, of course, they were speaking of waves.

"Ooooo, such priddy surfin' waves," said the one whose name was Awe F'shore.

"Aye, and a fine little nook t'be riding," responded Slyde, beginning with a laugh, then pulling up short as Frog sprang into the trail before them and

catapulted himself over the nose of the glass surfboard that Slyde carried under
his arm.

"Whoopiddy hey, y'Frog!" yelled Slyde. "Cuz why d'ya leap so strartly?"

Frog lay on his back in a bed of moss shaking with croaky little spasms, and
he could not answer, so hard was he laughing. For it was Frog's delight to upstart
travelers, especially surfers.

"He laughs and he laughs and he laughs, but nary a clue will he give us,"
said Reefe, the one with the kinky hair and the bright, bright blue eyes.

"Hey-oo," demanded Awe F'shore, nudging the giggling little green body
with a bare toe. "Tell us a'where this way goes!"

Frog stopped his laughter with much effort, gasping gradually back into an
understandable state. "Orkle," he said. "Orkle, orkle, orkle . . ." and then he was
off on another laughing spree.

"Water!" demanded Reefe, and the invocation of this one word immediately
gagged Frog's laughter. Water was the core word of the common language and,
by law, demanded acknowledgment in the real tongue, which was the language
of water.

"Grrnlick," began Frog, clearing his throat of the gravelish tones of his
species tongue. "This road leads t' theeg boundless OOOSun . . ." (by which
they named the ocean) " . . . erg leads toodeeg ghorsch orgdeeg OOOSun.
Ergleegs ywayvahg y'tergnal chrgghlgggh." Frog found himself hopelessly
tongue-tied, and Awe F'shore translated:

"He spoke of the way to the OOOSun, and how we will come to an island
wrapt by an unending wave—an y'ternal ywayvah faster and faster . . ."

"Around an island all twisty an' twisting, a loop diddy wave . . . ah," imagined
Slyde, his white eyes shining with wave fever. "Eternal wave . . . faster and faster!"

Beneath the gargantuan shaggy-barked arms of the huge forest with its infinite blossoms of fingertip darkness, the twisty-dusty road dipped and swayed.
Upon it the three surfers wended their way toward the sea, speaking excitedly in
the twilight of the shadowed sun, their bare feet churning the fine earth up and
around their knees in clouds.

An island around which waves peeled endlessly and somehow faster and
faster . . . how incredible! And yet Frog had spoken in the language of water, so
it must be so (it is quite impossible to lie in that particular language).

The pace was fast and steady and, whenever they passed through patches of sunlight, their colored glass surfboards flickered like prismatic crystal.

Awe F'shore carried a blue slider. Blue, the color of air, of breath, of sapphire, of sea.

Slyde carried yellow, the color of fire and sun, the color of gold and seed.

And Reefe carried red, the color of iron and sunset and blood (and also the color of wine).

They came out of the forest at sunset. The lights of a village sparkled in the lowest nest of the rolling foothills. Beyond the village, in the distance, they beheld the molten reflection of sheets of golden cloud transfused upon the open face of the sea, the OOOSun.

Now, in those days, it was not the habit of surfers to pass through the cities or even the villages, though, of the two, village was better than city. Usually surfers would simply avoid such an obstacle, keeping to the outskirts, traveling cross-country (which was quite a pleasant way to travel). But there was an urgency in this situation, or at least the hearts of the three were so convinced, and they chose to pass through the village under cover of night.

They crossed the open foothills as darkness grew and the stars began to dust the heavens. They met but few travelers on the road, and those passed quickly, hurrying blindly off into the night. Most of them were bent and stooped with their loads. Others, passing, looked with shut eyes from the windows of carts and carriages pulled by meebs, and they bestowed only the power of their scorn on the surfers.

In those days, meeb was a shortened term for a metalloid earth energy beast, a low-being used by the citizens to perform certain basic mechanical tasks, such as propulsion and powering factories. Meebs had dull, metallic skin, a variable number of arms and legs, no head, and no voice.

The insults and scorn of passersby were born patiently by the three surfers, who were aware that these people were victims of the Hypnotic Siege, which had long starved the citizens of their rightful food, making them as hungry and dangerous as mad dogs.

At last, the road snaked down to the gates of the village, and they made a point to enter at a swift and steady pace, projecting as best could an aura of destination, while radiating considerable power of presence. They passed through suffocating corridors of concrete and stone—everywhere square walls and square windows, square doors and square signs—bright and colorful signs that demanded their attention. They passed hundreds and thousands of meebs milling aimlessly in every street and alley, searching out bits of rock and stone to feed on until, apparently at random, they were herded into impromptu teams when a carriage needed pulling or some other work needed doing. The headless forms of the meebs bespoke their indentured servitude. Alas, they were slaves.

But they were not the only slaves. The very citizenry paraded boldly with eyes closed tight. They exchanged greetings on the streets, rounded up meebs, sat drinking in pubs, arrested other citizens, all with their eyes closed tight. (Though sometimes the eyes of a citizen being arrested would flicker open for an instant with the shock.)

It was a sad sight to see, yet what could be done? Many times before the three surfers had stopped to tell a citizen: "Hey you, but your eye isn't open!" only to receive an abrupt denial, insult, or clout. So now they hurried on with nothing else to be done. For the citizens could hear a wave, but they could never see one.

Near the middle of the village a few people caught scent of the surfers. "Vandals!" they shrieked, then fell on them most maliciously, pawing at them with contorted fingers. But the surfers kept them at bay with the sharp glass noses of their boards and told them that they were merely actors in a play (which was true) and this seemed to stall the citizens long enough for escape.

Outside of the village, the air grew larger again, though off to the sides of the road could be seen the flares that marked the night excavations, as citizens mined rocks from the earth to feed the meebs. Still, the three breathed the clean air with much relief and exchanged bright smiles in the moonless night.

Ere dawn they wearied and put aside the trek to lay away on a grassy hillock a small distance off the road. Here the grass was rich and thick and welcoming, forming perfectly to cushion their shapes, and they slept with the lush smell of life perfuming each breath.

More weary than they suspected, they awakened later than the sun, and then only to the delicate tumble of flower petals down their cheeks and unreal, crystalline voices. Field sprites danced in the dewy grass, clad only in transparent fragile lace, singing sweetly and promising all. But the three surfers had seen more than one dried-up soul who ventured to play in their gardens.

"Ooo-weee, pretty boys," they beckoned. "Ooo-plaaay pretty boys, ooo-weee." But the surfers made off with a fixed purpose, for so strong was the power of the sprites' need that only a clear head could free the surfers from them. Still, it was a long while before the webs of temptation ceased to tangle their attention, and longer still till the fine prick of their song once again allowed the filling of the moment with the power of presence.

Toward noon, the dusty little road came to a raging river and a decrepit old iron bridge. A black-and-white wooden barrier blocked the way and, as the three approached, a large brutish being clothed in leather and chain shambled out of a dingy booth and stood astride the road. His face was as contorted and twisted as the snarl of the rapids beneath his bridge, and he was filled with the power of greed.

"Aaarrrggghhh!" he bellowed. "Gristle thirst angrit unthrumble merfnill ambersought!"

But the surfers had no ambersought, and so were at a loss.

"Eenow y'passin happly nowee bindin," asked Slyde, hoping for a free passage.

"Aaarrrggghhh!" the collector wrenched once more from his throat and made a movement to take out his "mortifier," a device that snatched a chunk from a person's body if he resisted and drained his blood if he did not.

Instantly the three stepped backwards, lofted their prismatic glass sliders, and crossed them so that the sunlight passed through all three, blinding the lout with a blaze of white light. They danced around his whirling, frenzied efforts to lay hold of them and scampered swiftly over the hunchbacked bridge.

Now the way lay open to the OOOSun, and a cool breeze was at their backs. They followed the winding road past meadow and farmhouse, past sawmill and dairy, down towards the sea. They dipped down into a green, lush valley through which the wild river crashed and roared its way home, then at last they climbed a steep hill that brought them to the peak of a giant, bald headland.

Below them was the OOOSun. The headland and the point that it formed were triangularly shaped, though at some seaward point was a peculiar rock formation that resembled a huge stone seat or throne. Gathering in front of this rock formation and wrapping around the point on both sides were waves, and the three surfers let out hoot and hooray at the long-overdue sight.

Yet farther off the coast was an island, and to that they soon turned their gaze, hidden though it was in a shroud of mist.

Gull saw them the moment they came out into the clear. Three surfers. He was heading straight in from the island, tacking against a brisk offshore breeze. He coaxed his sleek form closer and closer till the three were almost directly below him, then he caught a downdraft and plummeted, nearly onto their heads. He hung motionless before their eyes, suspended in the warm wind, blinking from face to face to face and going: "Yawk! Yawk! Yawk!"

"Water!" said Reefe. "Is this the island of the unending wave?"

"Whorlen, whorlen, whorlen!" chortled Gull. "The vortex consumes itself and so lives forever!"

"How can we be getting to the island sooner than this?" asked Awe F'shore, who wanted to be there as soon as possible or faster.

"Y'fly it!" laughed Gull, then peeled off down one side of the headland.

Below them, the surfers could see a cluster of beings on the beach. They scampered down a weaving trail that brought them through delightful little gullies and glens, filled with flowers and shining colored stones, until they found themselves out on the warm white sand.

"Water," greeted Slyde, as they approached the group. They were clearly from a coastal tribe, that was certain, yet they seemed not to be nomadic, for their huts were permanent-looking, built back in the hollows at the base of the headland. Also, they did not appear too friendly, and a few even began to face around all squabblish and space-filling.

"Shoo! Shoo!" spat one, motioning at them severely to go back the way they had come. But the three held their ground.

"In common courtesy," spoke Reefe, "we implore you to befriend us!"

But the others, about eight in number, were local dwellers and would have none of it, nor would they speak in the language of water, a violation of the oldest and most sacred covenant.

"Grrdlycch!" demanded the leader of their group (who was called Storm Chop). His piercing black eyes, tangled black mat of hair, and twisted attitude made him quite disagreeable. "Smeernluggh!" he added.

Slyde tried to explain that the surfers were merely passing through, on their way to the island. There was no need to raise such a fuss, even if they had planned to surf this point (which, in truth, they were most anxious to do).

But still Storm Chop refused them. This was their beach, he gargled. And their waves. Go back to where you came from, he demanded. The villagers leave us alone as we are, but if you come here they will become aroused and dump huge rocks into our waves and snuff the passion from the sea (for as all surfers knew at that time, waves were the emotions of the deep).

The dwellers, therefore, refused to let them enter the water, and because violence among surfers was unthinkable, the three kept to the beach as they walked out to the point. Here they came upon the huge stone seat and saw that one of the dwellers appeared to be living in one of its higher crevices.

"Nyoo! Nyoo!" he scolded as they approached. "Skootooba, skootooba . . . nyoo!"

The surfers attempted to ignore his obscene language and the possessive sucking of his lips, which glistened with a vile green moisture. When the three managed to pass by the catlike pawing of his twisted fingers, a great fear seemed to overcome him, and he cowered back into his hole.

"Betoooom!" he warned. "Ya mort yallus!" No one ever goes up there, he said. A tomb for us all!

Yet, gaining the perch, the three enjoyed the finest of views and experienced a strong clear-headedness. They felt the beat of the sea as if they were atop some giant instrument or tuning fork, as gulls began to flutter and soar in from all directions. Then, quite instinctively, they felt a large set of waves approaching, and with no pause to think, they dove off the seat of the throne and plunged into the briny warmth of the welcoming OOOSun.

There was little time waiting, as the wave was on them almost before they could gain control of their glass sliders. It was a huge and hollow, yet somehow delicate, wall of water that looped and folded far over their heads as they paddled and tubed them before they could get to their feet.

"Ya-whooooooooo!" they wailed together, standing and turning hard like three parts of the same being. Reefe rode low, Awe F'shore rode high under the lip, and Slyde hugged the deepest center of the wave's pocket. They streaked along like this for some distance, then began to work the face, covering the wave with a lace of tracings, sometimes converging and passing at the same point, creating a brief, blinding flicker of white light before resuming their separate paths: red, yellow, and blue.

But the dwellers had paddled out to head them off! Six now took the drop on their emerald sliders, forming a wall that blocked the way of the three blazing surfers.

There was nothing else to be done. The three fell into line with one another: Reefe in the lead, then Awe F'shore and Slyde. Then Reefe stalled his slider and leaped into the air, so that Awe F'shore's slider slipped over his, and onto this he landed. Then, stalling the piggy-backed sliders, both leaped up as Slyde brought his yellow streaker over the other two. Then they were three together on a chariot of clear light. Time fused, and a message echoed outward. They passed through the line of dwellers like a bolt of lightning through a house of cards, and the gulls, hearing the message, swooped down by the thousands to carry off the dwellers.

As the huge wave continued to curl along the point, it grew more and more hollow and cavernous as it spun faster and faster, the three now surfing together — a single projectile in the barrel of the wave. Faster and faster, faster and faster . . . till the end loomed like a giant clamshell, and they rocketed off the lip, soaring hundreds of feet through the air and touching down halfway out to the island.

Here they dove into the water, disconnected the three surfboards, and lay down on their separate sliders again. Because the prismatic properties of their crystalline surfboards transformed solar energy into a vector, paddling was largely a way of steering. They sailed out toward the island as if swept along by a strong current.

The closer they came, the more their eyesight could penetrate the mist that forever surrounded the island. Soon it was plain that this mist was created by the endless churning of the waves, for the island was now close at hand and the roar and wail of perpetually collapsing waterforms filled all space with sound.

It took a while to find the lineup, but once in it the situation was clear. The waves marched in from the open sea, erupted over a perfect wedge-shaped reef, then wrapped and peeled around the entire island until they came back on, and were swallowed by, themselves. And as the waves completed their wrap, they went incredibly hollow, sucking out over exposed reef, and then merged once again with the takeoff point of a new wave, so that, for a period of several hundred feet there were two tubes, one within the other, forming a deep scooped-out bowl with a double-thick lip and no bottom.

So incredible were the possibilities that fear was no factor. The three surfers had tasted waves throughout the land, but never anything like this. Eagerly they took the drop: first Reefe, then Awe F'shore, then Slyde. It was an amazing ride to each of them: continually banking off an approaching bowl that never let down. They started with the sun at their backs, and soon they were coming full-face toward it.

The first time, coming around to the takeoff point and the bowl, Slyde looked ahead and saw Reefe bank high, high and around, perfectly perpendicular to the wave face. Then he saw Awe F'shore snap around the curve, locked into a tube within a tube nearly three times his height. And then, before he knew it, he felt as if he were being gathered in by some huge energy, and as he flew around the bowl, he had to flatten his stance to stay with his yellow glass slider. His white eyes streamed tears and his hair felt as though it would be pulled out of his head by the roots; his cheeks flapped with the velocity.

The second time through the bowl nearly flattened him. On the third go-around, he nearly lost consciousness. And then something changed . . .

Coming into the bowl for the fourth time, everything became suddenly slow and silent, as if a threshold had been crossed. There was no sound at all; it was a missing dimension, and each bead of water in the cascading wall was as clear and distinct as an ice cube.

And the island . . . it was no longer an island at all. It pulsated like a gigantic egg, stressed from within and glowing with the heat of some form of life ripe for emergence.

Barely moving now, the wall of water that stood beside Slyde was crystal clear and full of dolphins playing and laughing, though soundlessly. And far, far away he saw Awe F'shore. And further, further away there was Reefe. And beyond that he saw himself gazing into the wall of water at the dolphins.

A strange sensation came over Slyde, a sensation of being an echo. At first he thought that there was someone else on the wave behind him, above him. Perhaps a clear slider? But the answer came with the question, or so close on its heels there was no time to wonder: the wave, above all, broke for itself . . . spun around this island for itself.

And he was just a free rider. He could feel now—because of the change of speed—the actual emotion of the wave, and the emotion was the emotion of surfing.

The wave was surfing itself! This wave was feeling its own endless wrap of this island that was both an island and not an island. Indeed, it was an egg!

"Whorlen, whorlen, whorlen! . . . The vortex consumes itself and so lives forever . . ."

It was then that a sudden snap whipped through the bowl, breaking the orbit of Slyde's endless situation. His slider was shattered into stardust, and he was flung at the island. He exploded through the shell of the egg.

～

He hushed his croak and squatted back in the trees. Surfers were coming down the windy trail. He waited and watched till they came around the final bend and out into the light of the clearing. As they passed, he sprang out into the trail before them, then catapulted over the nose of one of the glass surfboards.

Something about this was so humorous that he lay in a clump of moss laughing hysterically, even though one of the surfers prodded him with a toe and shouted, "Hey-oo!"

"Orkle, orkle, orkle," he said, breaking again into uncontrollable giggles.

But then he was called to task by the irrefutable demand. "Water!" they commanded.

And so he cleared his froggy throat and told them of the way of the road and the "y'ternal ywayvah faster and faster" and chuckled to see the bulging excitement of their white eyes and the familiar departure.

Happily, Frog lay his long, green body back in the moss and waited patiently for the next beginning.

This story originally appeared in the December/January 1974–75 issue of Surfing *magazine and has been revised.*

a long-ago tale of
the birth of mystic eye

What is here told occurred exactly in that space of time which can, in no way, be located within the procession of the history which we know and in which we live. If you went backward, you would miss it, just as you would also miss it in going forward. Though it is here (as much as this is here, wherever you are), and what follows should be proof enough.

IT WAS WELL ON INTO SUMMER and the best ponds had dried hard, so that Frog had been forced to spring-flop, spring-flop, spring-flop down towards those cool, clear pools that bubbled up out of the ground in the valleys by the OOOSun. He had made this same journey before, three summers earlier (that was in the year of the rainless storms), but had returned in winter because something deeply magnetic in him knew that his place in the world was to wait beside the OOOSun road. There he directed the roving bands of surfers towards the y'ter-nal y'wayvah, thereby hastening and assuring his own eventual return to a surfer's role, perhaps even on a higher level than last time (though from Frog-stance, that was hard to imagine). Just getting back into a surfer's body would be perfection enough for his soul.

However, in such dry times there was no choice but to abandon his watch by the roadside and proceed to spring-flop his way down to the OOOSun. It was quite a giddy experience, as the relaxing, nonattached dallying in the mossy roadside and sampling the plethora of available taste treats had (over the three years since his last trek to the sea and back) rather distended his midmost points. In short, he was a fat Frog, and the spring-flop had, as a result, become much more flop than spring. And this, of course, aggravated another of Frog's innate characteristics, which was laughter. The spring was okay, but the flop sent spasms coursing through his electric green fat—pulses of ticklishness and waves of pure silliness. Invisible fingers seemed to poke at his ribs and jab at all his funnyspots.

The energy drain was enormous. He had been giggling for 466 gryphon strides and did not know if he could continue. Besides, he now found himself at a nice, shaded little pond (though the water had gone a little green and thick) that looked like it might have a few more weeks left in it.

So he rested. He found a sodden bed of moss beneath a miniature forest of maidenhair fern, stretched out his long, green legs, and rested his webbed feet on a large orange mushroom, then laid his head back on his folded webbed hands.

His dream was of his former life. Once again he rode the y'ternal y'wayvah faster and faster. Once again he crossed some threshold where everything slowed and the wave became a wall of crystal, and he looked ahead to see himself . . . and the island had become an egg, and the wave, he realized, was surfing itself, for itself; and then the sudden snap, whipping through the bowl, breaking the orbit of his endless situation, shattering his slider into stardust, and flinging him towards the island and through the shell of the egg, which is where all this had begun. And then he had awakened to find himself Frog.

Frog, as in a fairy tale, and now each time he heard the sound of water there was that strange, mystic current that cut through wherever he was at the moment, as if the sound of water was the whispering of another world. That sound would turn him back on himself, fill him with a longing nostalgia, which at first he sometimes failed to recognize—just something familiar—and then he would remember: water. The sound of water. The sound of . . . water!

He blinked open his mucoused eyes. The sound of water, soft and delicate, played in his ears, stirring the memory of his journey . . . and the meaning of it . . . reminding him. He lifted his head above the dry grass.

There was a being by the pond, a female human dressed in the coarse gray uniform of the common citizenry. She had removed a boot and was dabbling at the thick, green water with her foot.

The delicate sound of her toes in the water, along with the pathetic angle of her posture, stirred feelings of remorse and nostalgia in Frog. She was obviously, like the other citizens of the town, a victim of the Hypnotic Siege. Her form was a bit crooked, twisted and hunched, and as she stooped and turned to take off the other boot, Frog could see that her eyes were sealed shut and her face bore that pained frown that characterized the souls of the new age. Still, he sensed she was more alive than most he had seen.

He would have wished to enjoy the waters himself now, but he could not go near a citizen, for his instincts knew that they did not respect their own lives, let alone the life of a meager Frog. So he was forced to squat impatiently in the rough, dry grass, waiting for her to leave, while the hot sun baked and dried his amphibian skin to leather.

Along about the time he was beginning to feel that he might not even have the strength to croak, there was a rustle of grass and the padding of bare feet. The female drew her feet up suddenly out of the water and froze in an expectant crouch.

A surfer (Frog recognized Awe F'shore) skipped nimbly down to the edge of the pond, set down his crystal blue glass slider, knelt, and began to spread away the surface scum with his hands to drink. He hunched over, seemed to study the reflection of his face momentarily, then looked up suddenly without drinking. He saw the female.

For a long moment they studied one another across the pond, each frozen in the control of their instinctive reactions to the other. Impatience gnawed at Frog. "Y'pond'll bee dryup afore yee moovit!" he screeched under his breath, though there was something comical in it all that made him giddy with wanting to orkle.

At last Awe F'shore rose to his feet and began cautiously to move around the pond, not taking his eyes off the female, who in turn merely cowered further up into a ball, her nose twitching at his approach.

Awe F'shore came to where she was and walked around her at a distance, studying her, drawing closer, then further away. It seemed to be a dance of attraction and repulsion; he could not decide what to do, and he could not leave either.

Usually the nomadic surfers avoided citizens unless it was absolutely necessary to deal with them. They never knew how they would react. Sometimes they could be civil, at times almost friendly. And then, for no observable reason, they might become angry, even violent. Surfers had been run out of area after area, herded out into the deserted and uncharted coastal territories. Some had been imprisoned and forced to mine stones for the meebs (the headless, metalloid erg-servers of the masses).

And the most sure way for a surfer to arouse the impulse of violence in the citizens was to be seen with their children, especially their daughters.

And here was Awe F'shore courting certain disaster, stalking even such a possibility, moving with each revolution closer and closer to where she sat, shaking now, at the edge of the pond.

Finally, he stopped beside her and dropped to his knees. He carefully reached out and touched her cheek. She jerked away and trembled; her nose quivered like a spring rabbit.

Fascinated, Frog scooted closer to have a look and a listen.

"OOOwee but choo are sooo priddy!" exclaimed Awe F'shore. "Priddy 'n' moor in a laydee citysin than e'er have I seen!"

"Baffadda ugprennt!" she snarled at him, but his hand continued to gently stroke her cheek, and she quieted. Soon they were so much absorbed in one another that Frog was able to drag his crispy green body to the pool and slide stealthily in.

Entering this other world was much like when he had entered the world of a Frog. You only saw the surface of it before, and now you were in it, and the world you left behind grew quiet and was soon forgotten. All is immediately cool and buoyant, and you quickly forget that you were ever parched by the wicked noon sun.

When he emerged refreshed from the pond, Frog could see neither the surfer nor the female citizen. He left the pond reluctantly, but he knew that it was shrinking and doomed—in a few days he would have to leave it anyway. He knew that leaving now was best, before the days became even hotter. The summer solstice, the longest day of the year, would soon arrive.

The road down to the OOOSun was dry and treacherous, and Frog encountered many evil creatures that savored his precious bag of juices. But, though he was a Frog, there was something in him still that knew how to think and move as a surfer, and that made all the difference. In his ancient surfer's cortex, each dangerous encounter was a sucked-out, collapsing section of wave, and only by taking the surest, cleanest, most precise path could he escape. And this, much to his enlarging delight, is exactly what he was able to do.

Six hard days took him across the Sand Inferno Valley. Three more days to spring-flop through Suboobia. Two weeks to scale and descend the Loose Ambulance Unnatural Foulest Mountains, with scarce a wet stone upon which to cool his tongue and imbibe refreshment. Oh, it was sheer terrible!

It was a drastically parched and thirsty Frog that descended that final slope to the azure bed of mother OOOSun, spread out below like the cheek of the fairest blue maiden.

He found a deep, cool shoreline pool where fresh water bubbled up between stone crevices surrounded by cooling evergreens. Here he plunged into the satisfying deeps and later rested on fat, green lily pads and unctuous beds of moss. Why had he ever left, he asked himself, knowing full well he had been chosen to live by the road and direct the surfers to their y'ternal y'wayvah. If he failed in that task, how could he hope to return again to the life of a surfer?

As it happened, a tribe of surfers lived nearby (as they have always done at this place, where there is a five-mile-long, perfect sand-bottomed point), and each day the men, women, and children would come up from the dunes and bathe in the fresh water. Frog saw many that he knew and one that he knew differently—Slyde—the one who had taken his place in this life. Perhaps he had been the Frog last time.

On the afternoon of his third day at the pool, Frog overheard a disturbing conversation. Some exceptional argumentation passed between the surfers, such that the word "Water" had to be spoken three times to quell it. The point of discussion turned on the involvement of one of the surfers with a citizen and his intent to bring her here to the beach on the following day. Another of the surfers denied consent and condemned this proposal.

Awe F'shore (for it was he that so wished and was so challenged) replied it was no one's business but his own. The other surfer said it was everyone's business because the citizens would follow her here and drive them off the beach. Awe F'shore said the citizens could go ride the Mafazoomian shorebreak for all he cared . . . and so on. Finally, it was determined that Glascurl, chief of this nomadic coastal tribe, would decide.

Frog began to fear strongly for Awe F'shore—not only for force of judgment which the challenge would focus on him, but for his basic sanity. Because Frog knew that a free rider of the OOOSun's tempestuous emotions must be free of the Dog Hunger and thus protected from entanglements with victims of the Hypnotic Siege.

Frog remembered his own past-life treks through the towns and villages on his way to the y'ternal y'wayvah—the blind citizens lurching through the filthy streets, acting out their miserable life stories as if their eyes were open instead of closed. He remembered the headless metalloid meebs, gobbling stones in the alleyways, corralled into mindless servitude—pulling carriages, hauling cargo, and performing the many filthy and thankless tasks that fell to the subspecies that provided the requisite energy by which the citizens could continue to live in their own subhuman states. And now Awe F'shore wished to bring one of these citizens here to live with him!

The following day, a great crowd pressed in around the deep, still pool, and no one was allowed to disturb the waters. Awe F'shore had resolved to bring in this citizen in direct defiance of Glascurl's pronouncement that only those who bore surfing deep in their true essence could join the coastal tribe. The very soul of the tribe was at stake, and the tribe had gathered here at the pool, by which the road passed, to present a solid wall of resistance to the interloper.

Now, it was essential to the code of all coastal peoples that there should never be violence between surfer and surfer. If there was, then all participating individuals were turned out into the world of the living dead, and their knowledge of the language of water was stripped from them by the conjoined emanations of their fellow tribesmen. In other words, they entered the world of the dying living, a twilight zone between the surfers and the citizens.

This same punishment might also come to one who defied a direct judgment of the tribal chief, spoken in the language of water and sealed with the invocation of the Infinite Curling Moment.

So it was that when Awe F'shore came trudging steadily down the mountain trail, his hand holding that of the citizen female, who stumbled along behind, Frog felt the greenest he had ever felt, this life or last. He slithered in amongst all the bare feet and crouched at the pool's edge to watch and listen.

"Be holden, Awe F'shore!" commanded Glascurl, standing tall and powerful above the others. "Water! No kin yee passe, for have we betold yee nay citysin can wee have withus here. Water!"

"Kinyee noot see that she issnay o' the kind o' t'other citysins yonder?" pled Awe F'shore.

"Nay . . . Water," said Glascurl. "Owr code issclear an' closes out 'pon her as ever on an'other."

"Nay!" challenged Awe F'shore, showing uncustomary impatience for a surfer who had ridden through the greatest of the holy water chambers. "She issnay o' the kind o' t'other citysins!"

Glascurl considered where a just solution might lie. In the end, setting new precedent, he allowed that the citizen female could speak to that barefooted assembly. And so she stepped just forward of Awe F'shore, standing on the road before the expectant tribe at the edge of the deep still pool of Water and Truth. Her blind eyelids trembled, her body was twisted and pained. Her voice, unlike the melodious timbre of Awe F'shore and Glascurl and the others, reflected harshly off the water, yet there was something wistful in her, Frog felt. So he tried very hard to listen carefully to her, though the listening was, in truth, painful.

"Ngsurfnem! Argnglich armnigast pgghunge lphyrtzt. Grdnooffg lampght tylpwsq lhgyterg! Grmmwaynahjg oooooooghtyyyryt losssss! Pleagse! Lrggh! Lrgghvvg! Loughve! Love! Warghh! Warghhtergh! Water!"

A wave of amazement swept through the tribe. Never before had a citizen pronounced the word Water to them. Never had they heard the throat of a citizen speak of Love. Granted, she had struggled and twisted it out of herself, but still . . .

The emotions of the surfers were now bent from their stern resolve. Something in the female had reached out and touched them. They looked at Glascurl expectantly to see how he was affected.

Glascurl considered for several long moments what to do. He studied the female, then studied his heart, and then his mind, where the code of the coastal tribe was held. Finally he declared this an Infinite Curling Moment and pronounced his judgment: to test the life of the female's essence-self, she would be taken out to the reef when the swell was next above ten feet, and there she would have the chance to demonstrate the validity of her claim to a space within their tribe.

The tribe dispersed in a low roar of excitement, as Awe F'shore retired with the female back up the road to wait by a smaller pool for the conch to blow the arrival of waves.

Well refreshed and back to greenormal, Frog leaped buoyantly up the trail after them and never missed a thing that passed between the two. He heard her speak of the life in the town under the Hypnotic Siege: how her family did not know one other, how they ate each other's energy and possibilities, how the meebs rusted and decayed everywhere, how the most ignorant became the most successful, and how without eyes it was impossible to tell what was truly beautiful from what was merely pretending to be. She told how her parents crushed her with their hunger for lies, and how they talked of surfers as being wicked and blind, which made Awe F'shore laugh, so ironical was it.

Frog also learned that Awe F'shore had come in the night for her, had taken her from her bed in the village, while her father sat right there at the table eating a gruel of chemical stew. And he heard that somewhere in her she seemed to bear another set of memories and that, quite surprisingly, she understood the concept of color even though she could not see.

Finally one day the conch blew, and Frog was hard-pressed to keep up with the girl and Awe F'shore as they raced down the road toward the shore. For her test, Awe F'shore had fashioned a fine crystal slider of an unknown color.

On the beach the tribe had gathered, and others from further up the coast had also come, knowing sooner of the swell. The crowd parted as Awe F'shore and the female citizen passed through, with the ever-curious Frog springing after them like a grasshopper.

The swell was better than ten feet. It was nearly twenty, and some of the waves did not hold, but collapsed in huge sections. Yet Awe F'shore knew there was nothing else to be done. He set her board in the channel and helped her onto it; then he laid down on his own board to accompany her out to the lineup, where the immense peaks quivered and exploded into thundering white avalanches.

Once there, as the test demanded, he could not interfere nor say anything except "Water" and watch her take on the task. For a long time she sat unmoving as the great waves passed beneath, lifting her high, then setting her down. She was feeling the rhythm. He could see her organizing her understanding.

And then there came a huge wave, and Awe F'shore spun and moved away, out to sea to escape, thinking she would do the same, but forgetting for a moment she could not see. And when he turned and looked back, he saw her sitting beneath the huge curl of the wave, darkened in its overhanging shadow. He was just about to cry out, violating the rule of the test, when she lay forward onto her slider and began to fall down the face of the mighty wave.

The rest, of course, is familiar to all coastal people who have been brought up on the great tales of those days: How she dropped down and down and further down still, how she stood, shakily at first, on the crystal slider, the wind whipping at her hair and smoothing away the deformities of her face, how her body came upright and bold, how the speed and something else pulled tears out of the corners of her eyes, and how soon they opened on the colors of the world, and how when they did she was deep back inside a twenty-five-foot perfect wave. And how she emerged from the maw far inside the bay to the cheers of those on the beach.

As the story goes, at first, no one could believe that it was actually her, so changed was she by that wave!

That was when we first learned that sometimes you cannot tell. Sometimes the victims of the Hypnotic Siege are surfers who do not know it. Like Mystic Eye (for that became her name), they are possessed as babes and programmed into a life of darkness and oblivion, yearning forever for a world of color and life that they simply know exists, but cannot see.

For Frog (once the rains had come again and bathed the parched lands), the trip back to the OOOSun road and his station beside it was filled with wonders. Somehow, he was seeing the world anew once again . . . simply because Mystic Eye now saw it differently.

Hence, too, whenever a citizen would accidentally stumble onto the road to the y'ternal y'wayvah, Frog would be sorely tempted to leap across their path and point them on the way. After all, there was always a chance that some of them, deep inside, knew the way already.

This story first appeared in Surfing *magazine in 1975 and has been revised.*

peace and war

IT'S ONLY FICTION.

I arrived in M_____ on Monday evening, the 10th of September, 2001. Loaded my gear into the trunk of a beat-up taxi and headed straight for the Doriat, a cheap hotel with a penchant (otherwise unknown in these parts) for clean sheets and fresh towels. The ceiling fan spun me into dreams of insect armies on the move, gruesome dismemberments, and pools of awful blood. I awoke in the dark, sweating, went looking for a clean, well-lighted place, and found the Pi'sto Aristo open to the damp predawn air, a few besotted patrons glued to some overblown disaster movie.

I ordered a Bloody Mary and sat at the bar, savoring the cool tomato juice braced with the clear spirit of vodka, the heat of pepper. The movie played in the mirror, and I looked away. The skinny bartender watching, transfixed, gave me not a glance as he said, "Tear wrists . . . new walk traits enter . . . hair play crosh . . . es plote." Then I noticed the onscreen logo—CNN—and something in my chest caved in.

The thirteenth, the world teetering on the edge of Armageddon and Apocalypse, found me aboard a hired prahu (basically a proa). The morning dank and slick. The smell of it gave me an overpowering sense of doom, feelings of foreboding. Not a breath of wind. We motored out of the harbor like Imperialists. The captain and owner of this wreck, burly and as Islamic as I was Southern California SUV Surf—grinned with his mouth and teeth, but not with his eyes. He aimed to kill me, I was convinced. I had been given his name by a friend who had never met him, who got it through a local and (I now realized) very primitive booking agency. According to the documents, his name was M. Suta.

The mate (just the three of us aboard) was a skinny, black-eyed island boy scantily dressed in the ruins of American sportswear. He seemed nervous. His face appeared emotionally bruised and volatile, mobile with expression—now tender and vulnerable, now dull but sinister.

I was uneasy, but I held an optimism that all was basically well with the world, and that if I behaved with strength and composure and good cheer, they would honor our arrangement. Even so I gathered my gear around me on the filthy deck and, sweating profusely, began to collect the most important items into a small pack that I would keep with me at all times.

Beyond the rip-rap breakwall, the sea was smooth as gelatin, burnished a pale ochre by a dirty haze. Volcano weather, if you believed the lore. The boat was slow. The 4-knot breeze brought little relief from the heat. We were headed for V_____, a small island in a remote archipelago known for quality surf and a mellow population of seagoing natives. There was no "tourist industry"—not yet anyway—and really no way to get there except this way, or with your own boat, which was how my friends had arrived a month earlier.

I had planned to be with them, but the sale of my company (a one-man outfit that produced emergency software for holographic applications), which was actually the celebratory inspiration for the trip, was delayed when the lead man for the acquisition team (proving that truth is stranger than fiction) was seriously injured by a shark. The guy (Gary Laughlin) wasn't a surfer, he was a recreational diver. He got caught in a heavy rip off the Farallon Islands with a bag of abs and blew right into the jaws of a Great White. He swung the bag around just in time to basically stuff the thing down the shark's throat, but both his arms were stripped of massive amounts of skin and tissue in the extrication process. Luckily his major plumbing was intact. He spent almost three hours in the water (bleeding!) before his buddy found him. A shot of the Coast Guard helicopter plucking him out of the Boston Whaler made all the national TV news.

To make a long story short, I said good-bye to three of my best friends at the Santa Cruz boat harbor and watched them literally sail off into the sunset. That was in May, almost four months earlier. They'd had a great crossing, not without an adventure or two, and arrived at V_____ in mid-August. They'd been getting good surf ever since, while I was going nuts.

And then one day I was on a plane headed halfway around the world to meet my buddies. They were anchored off a small island among a scattering of other small islands in a tropic sea. The deal was done, my business was sold, the business I'd started six years earlier, the business I'd cleverly named for that famous emergency telephone number: 911.

Late Friday morning, Suta steered *Nab-i-Lat* into a small, unexceptional lagoon and brought her to a stop in deep water a hundred feet or so off a nondescript island. He idled the foul little engine while the mate (the captain called him something like "Drak") cranked the rotting punt down from its rusting davits until it sat on the water below. I scanned the scene—no sign of the others, no boat, no buildings or huts. Just palms and a low jungly underbrush fringing the white sand.

"Are you sure this is the place?" I asked. Drak was reaching up for my bags, rubbing his bony fingertips together with impatience. I lowered the two big bags, then the three boards. Suta ignored us, looking around at the other islands, up at the clouds, at his watch, the sun, the smoke of the diesel's exhaust.

"Is this V____?" I demanded of the captain. He nodded sharply two or three times without looking my way, motioning with a downward push of his left hand that I should descend the decomposing jute ladder, which I did. I still remember the smell of it, like salt, nori, and creosote.

The mate stood in the wobbling punt and poled the shallow-bottom boat tentatively in over the shallow reef until he'd beached its square bow into the coral with a pronounced crunch. I strapped on my reef-walkers and stepped over the side into a couple of feet of warm water between mounds of brain coral. It felt delicious. I gathered up two boards and waded gingerly to the beach, itself a coarse litter of pummeled reef. As I returned for the rest of my stuff, the punt was shrinking rapidly towards the prahu and Mr. M. Suta.

I'm not a bad swimmer. I almost caught them. It wasn't until Suta laughed that I knew he had me beat, and by then the water was full of sharks. I had swum into a cloud of baitfish and jack, and beautiful silver blacktips were boring holes in the formation, snapping and gulping as they flew past me. They didn't seem to be interested in me, it was the jack they were after, and I managed to make it back to the beach without an unpleasant incident.

The beach was empty, the lagoon was deserted, and they (the *Nab-i-Lat* just then rounding the northeast corner of the island) had my food and water. It was the first time in my life I felt exactly that way—sort of a larger version of how you might feel if you'd just locked yourself out of your car in a Rio backstreet.

I couldn't afford to be angry; I was in too deep. The beach stretched in a smooth arc along the shallow crescent of the lagoon. A walk around the island took less than ten minutes, so it was about a half mile. There were islands to the north, east, and west—open ocean to the south. The lagoon was on the north side.

I scrambled through the middle of the island and after about 50 yards (144 feet to be exact) emerged on the south side, where a hollow scoop of bay curved out to a low, rocky headland. It was a great setup for surf, might actually be V_____, except there were no mellow seagoing natives and no sign of Roy, David, and Leslie or the *Lorenzo*. Wondering what to do, I watched a foot-high wave curling towards me down the west side of the bay.

There were plenty of coconuts. The long, narrow east side of the island was almost a monoculture of coconut, although it bore no organized resemblance to a plantation. Some thick-leafed bushes nested in the brighter areas, and they were loaded with small pepper-shaped fruits that tasted like guava.

The west end was volcanic and elevated, rising all of twelve feet, and the bouldering was defined against the grassy terrain out where the headland tumbled off into large black boulders off the south point. This side of the island was larger—a jagged square or oval populated by nut trees and passion vines. By contrast, the east end seemed to be a sandpit, supported along its south shore by another, smaller outcropping of rock.

The west end faced into a prevailing wind, towards the nearest island, lower and more spare than this one. Not a sail or boat in sight. The sea dark blue and deep. No structures of any kind. Only palms to gauge size and distance. This western shoreline was rocky except for a strip of white sand fringing a tiny natural harbor tucked into the south end of the headland, bounded by nearly submerged rocks that strained all the energy from the surf and left a pool of dappled calm. Within a week I'd created a regular path around and through all of this. Eventually it seemed like a highway.

I had a 6-foot 6-inch Rusty and an 8-foot Hamilton. The Rusty had traction, but the big board needed wax. I had two bars of tropical surf wax. I had two board bags, a key for the tri-fins and an allen wrench for the single. A 6-foot 6-inch leash and an 8-foot leash. I had a rash guard and towel in the pocket of each board bag, replacement fins all around, plus a pair of Churchill fins and a Hawai'ian sling.

I wore boardshorts, a T-shirt, reef-walkers, and a company hat (that "911" again).

In the daypack I had trunks, a T-shirt, a third towel, a dive mask and snorkel, Leatherman multitool, compass, 100 yards of duct tape, 100 feet of quarter-inch nylon line, 250 feet of cotton string, 500 feet of 10-pound-test monofilament, a wallet-sized tackle box with a dozen fishhooks, sinkers, floaters, and a few plastic lures, a small plastic sewing kit, one pair of sunglasses, two tubes of SPF-35 lotion, a tube of Bondo, a tube of shampoo, a block of soap in a Zip-lock bag, 100 water-purification pills, 100 chloroquine tablets, a pack of double-edged razor blades, a fishing knife, a Swiss Army knife (with two blades and a variety of tools including corkscrew, toothpick, and tweezers), a small spiral notebook, a No. 2 pencil with eraser, a Bic pen, compact Nikon binoculars, a Nikonos camera (with only the one 36-exposure roll inside—the rest of the film was in the large bags), my wallet, my toilet kit, a small first-aid kit, a plastic bottle of hydrogen peroxide, a half dozen plastic trash bags with ties, three Clif Bars (peanut butter), a Bic lighter, a film can of wooden matches, a tin of Altoids, and another tin filled with an assortment of items, including straight pins, safety pins, paper clips, guitar picks, some cash and a few coins, and the fortune from a cookie I'd picked up from the bar at Pi'sto Aristo, which read: What is the sound of one hand clapping?

Twenty feet off the beach, over a ridge of coral, the lagoon looked deep, rich, and ominous. Its blue was dark and opaque, as thick as paint on a canvas. But it burst into a froth of fine white bubbles when I dove over the edge and began to follow the wall down. For all intents and purposes, the lagoon was bottomless, since I was only good for about twenty feet at the most. Even so, it was clear that I wasn't going to starve.

The wall was like the apartment scene in Fellini's Satyricon, pocked with holes and hollows, almost every one an occupied apartment—lobster, eel, urchin, grouper, octopus, snail—and the lagoon itself was thick with bait fish, a hundred kinds of sierra, jack, barracuda, shark, and millions of reef fish. Within five minutes I was picking my way carefully up onto the reef with a bleeding five-pound jack, a step ahead of the sharks.

I had set up my camp in the lee of the headland, tucked back against a tumble of large boulders under a nut tree. The point was just out front, framed by a weeping roof of fronds, but there was no surf. Curiously, there were no animals on the island either, not even rodents, just the occasional seabird.

I cooked over a fire pit that I'd framed with alternating chunks of black rock and white coral. I drank the liquor and ate the flesh of delicious windfall coconuts. To collect fresh water, I built a kind of cistern nearby—a hole in the sand, about two feet deep, lined with a plastic bag, and covered with shingled leaves that drained the rain to the center. This proved quite effective, since it poured almost every night.

Each morning, then several times a day, I walked around the island, searching the surrounding waters through the binoculars. A trail now led through the palms to the north shore and the lagoon, where I had prepared the requisite signal fire, but it was always damp. I wished I had a mirror, but I never saw anything anyway. Still, I was relatively comfortable, relatively well-fed, relatively safe . . . for about a week. Then came the terror—fueled by sudden, graphic recollections of the images I'd seen on television in M_____, playbacks of jets exploding into towers, people flailing in the air as they fell a quarter mile, monumental landmarks imploding into great clouds of ash. These images seemed to contain much more detail than what I'd actually witnessed, and this detail only increased over time.

My imagination went to war—a war waged in utter isolation. It was a war of conflicting vision, cross-purposes, and lethal power. I was already lost, but now I began to lose my soul.

Late one afternoon, I wrote in the notebook: "One way or the other, life requires you to be a warrior." Then I went over to the west side and watched the sun melt, smearing the ruffled sea with gore. Darkness sucked away the daylight. Planets and stars poked holes in heaven. Black thoughts coalesced around brilliant images.

I had been in a repressed state of panic since the five Supreme Court "justices" elected George W. Bush, an individual of apparently modest intelligence, as President of the United States, even though he'd lost the election by over half a million votes. I knew just enough history to be dangerous to myself, and this knowledge fed a hideous fascist nightmare that seemed utterly believable. I knew that George W.'s grandfather, Prescott Bush, father of 43rd U.S. president George Herbert Walker Bush, was one of the directors of Brown Brothers, Harriman, an American financial institution that bankrolled the Nazis from 1925 until they were shut down for "trading with the enemy in 1942," almost a year into World War II.

I knew that our 43rd president himself had been CIA director in the '70s and was widely recognized as an architect of Central American oppression, death squads, cocaine trafficking, and all the rest of the sordid business. I knew a little about the Iran-Contra affair, the seesaw backing of Iran and Iraq, and the persisting irony of our government's support of dictatorial despots around the world.

During long, dark nights I sweat fear for the accumulating logic of this vision, remembering the McCarthy era, then Ike, then the Kennedy assassinations and Martin Luther King's. And for some reason I remembered the fall of The Wall in Berlin—November 9, 1989—on the Nazi high holy day of Blutzeuge, the Blood Witness, Hitler's favorite holiday, last celebrated in 1944.

I recalled the OPEC crisis of the winter of 1973–74 and the environmental incentives that came out of it with visions of alternative energy and sustainability. But then, twenty-five years and one Gulf War later, our SUVs were swollen metaphors of collective greed, and national ad campaigns once again depicted 4WD monsters chewing through nature's most perfect refuges as if the world was an American theme park.

I'd seen television, too, and knew that some CIA-trained Taliban "fanatic" was likely tuning into *Jerry Springer*, *Howard Stern*, and *Sex and the City* to see what America was up to, and no way do they want that in their backyard! Was it so hard to see why they saw the West as Satan? It wasn't exactly rocket science. Islam was fading from the world in direct proportion to the shrinkage of its oil reserves. What was so hard to understand? What could possibly stand in the way of Apocalypse now?

An infinitely layered sound—rush upon rush upon rush—woke me to hot sun slanting in on my tormented carcass. It had been another rough night. But it was gone now, erased again and again and again . . . as wave after wave wrapped into the bay and surged up onto the beach in front of me.

I paddled out into a dream. The water was lucid, riffled with a sentient texture—surely it was alive!—spinning elliptic curls down the point towards me. I looked in on them, over their shoulders. I surfed. I rode wave after wave after wave, and the experience transformed me. I don't know how else to put it. Folded into the rhythms of the world, I marveled. Sliding on liquid echoes. How could this be anything but miraculous? It was miraculous. How could this universe be anything less? How could it be anything other than perfect?

The passage of energy through matter organizes matter. What better way to see it than surf? Ride waves. Chaos, eternally bifurcating, but always organized into waves. The bloodlight of a setting sun is waves. So is the instinctive logic of fear, the cycle of the seasons, the patterns of societies and relationships. The wind is waves, these words are waves, and a wave is a wave. That's how it is.

I heard the ultimate question: Why is there anything? The answer at last: Because something is happening. Further and deeper reason cannot go, though everyone pretends. But something from further and deeper comes through, and it always comes through in waves, breaking into existence. Waves is how reality happens. That's how it was.

Once that swell hit, it stayed a good long time—24/7 for weeks. Sometimes bigger, sometimes smaller, but—two feet to eight feet—always there. Utterly hypnotic.

I was in a hypnotic dream of perfection. I ate, slept, and surfed, utterly fulfilled in the present. Dreaming the now—that's how it seemed.

One afternoon (it was getting late, the sun low, and I hadn't caught a fish for dinner yet), I was paddling back out for another last wave when it hit me that the dark thoughts—murder, torment and pain, disaster and ruin—were no less dreams, no less conspiracies of sleep and blindness, than the positive thoughts. Failures of vision, these dark thoughts made hope hopeless by failing to drink at the undulating well of the present. Somehow all of this, along with the wave riding, began to fill me with a profound optimism.

Like the sun and the moon (both of which I now knew more intimately than I could have imagined possible), these disparate entities, light and dark, orbited my consciousness, and if I stayed in the present, I could see them both. I could even see the confluence of massively accelerating environmental and social forces as the organic and correct unfolding of human nature, a test of the human species with concomitant transformational possibilities and opportunities.

If it sounded biblical, I realized that it was. The situation was challenging all of our boundaries, pushing us past all of our limitations. However narrow, we were being stretched, and the broadest of us were broadening even further.

On the one hand I saw that the outcome was obvious. Good would triumph over evil, and it had nothing to do with the United States of America or the United Nations or NATO or any "civilized" entity. It had nothing to do with terrorists or madmen or Islam. It had to do with consciousness, plain and simple. If the world was to survive—the world of humans, that is—the most conscious, aware, and honest among us had to rise up and drag the rest with them. People—we—would have to wake up. We'd have to find a truly sustainable plan that admitted to the realities of our situation—organic beings trapped together on a planet in outer space. Tearing each other apart, blowing each other to bits, burning each other with poisons . . . it was all so utterly medieval and ancient, so utterly wasteful.

"On the other hand," came the thought (it was night, the rhythmic surf chant filling the bay and my hut), "there are way too many people on Earth. Maybe this is the best way to get rid of a whole bunch of us."

Walking the beach alone (always alone!) I pondered this great population purge, the great battle of Armageddon, East and West devouring each other in the name of Allah and oil-fueled Capitalism, like a snake eating its own tail.

I looked around, alone as Adam, and saw no conflict. But I knew that—far from my island (and I truly felt it was my island by then)—one of these visions (or some other) was playing out, or maybe it was already finished. Perhaps the air I breathed was heavy with billions of lost souls.

Riding a wave one morning, I wondered. Where are the great poets of our time? Where are the spirits that will lift our spirits? I wondered. I had seen our leaders—presidents and generals. I knew their visions.

Is it every woman for herself and every man for himself? Or do we share a kind of "morphic field?" If so, can our so-called "collective unconscious" simultaneously conceive a sustainable future and lift us towards it? What about our collective consciousness? I wondered.

Watching the sun lift over the eastern horizon one morning, I wondered. How could these Taliban—these emirs of repression and perversion—have sprung from the same seed as Omar Khayyam and the mighty Rumi? What's wrong with them? Are they asleep in a dark dream of mythic hatred, or are they simply the last of the displaced nomadic peoples, backs against the wall of extinction?

If truth—make that: Truth—has power, then what is the Truth? What is the Truth of the current situation? Wherein lies its resolve? I wondered, knowing that resolution was working itself out somewhere beyond all my horizons.

Years went by. I lost interest in how many. Certainly more than one.

Boats had gone past in the distance—I don't know how many. Signal fires were lit, smoke sent aloft, but no one ever came. Who knows how many sailed close by that island while I was fishing or surfing on the opposite side? Once, perhaps a year after I'd been stranded, I discovered two sets of footprints, a litter of beer cans, some cigarette butts, and a few spent matches on the beach by the lagoon not fifty feet from my heaped-up burn pile and the chunks of coral spelling HELP.

But one afternoon there was a boat, an old proa not unlike the one that left me there, but crowded with a ragged assortment of islanders, none of whom spoke English, French, or German.

Be patient, I told myself, as we were heading back towards civilization. Time will tell.

But time wasn't talking. I watched the wave curling a crystal sheet back off the bow of the boat, endlessly shattering into foam. I imagined Confucius asking me the question, "What is the sound of one hand clapping?"

"Well," I answered, "it takes two hands to clap."

This story first appeared in the January 2002 edition of The Surfer's Path.

kaena point

Hawai'i, island of Oahu. Robust white clouds drift under true blue sky. Tall palms sway in soft afternoon breeze. The ocean is not far away.

On the fourth anniversary of the Japanese attack on Pearl Harbor—December 7, 1945—Lee Sizemore steps out through the gate of Scofield Barracks and onto Kunia Road to wait for the shuttle to town. He has just been discharged from the United States Army. Japan surrendered 113 days earlier, and now Lee is a free man—in Hawai'i.

He was born in Kansas City, Missouri, in 1924 and grew up nearby, mostly in a little town called David (pop. 1,326). A week ago, November 30th, was his twenty-first birthday. He was a radioman in the 25th Infantry Division and saw action in Guadalcanal, the Solomon Islands, and the Philippines. He saw misery and death. He made friends and lost them. He had always planned to head back to the mainland, but he'd stopped over here on the way out and liked it, so he transferred back to Scofield for release. He liked the smell here in Hawai'i, there was no death in it. It made him want to stay.

"Tropic lightning," the shuttle driver comments, reading his insignia as Lee boards. "Welcome home."

Watching out the window as the bus rolls down toward Honolulu, he feels at home in his tan uniform with the staff sergeant stripes, but this will be the last day he wears it. Let out on Hotel Street, he passes tattoo parlors, bars, Chinese apothecaries, shops with flowered silk shirts in the window . . . merchants and shoppers and whores.

He wanders down to the shoreline and finds himself at the harbor. Out on Sand Island, a Seabee crew is disassembling antiamphibious pylons, rolling up razor wire. He takes a cab out towards Diamond Head, sees a sign pointing inland, and tells the driver to stop. He rents an upstairs apartment in a two-story period piece on Koa Avenue between Uluniu and Kaiulani, a short block inland from Kalakaua and the beach called Waikiki, which the natives seem to pronounce "why-KEE-kee."

Pocketing the new key (the unit number "4" written on a brass-trimmed circular paper tag and tied to it with string), he walks down Kaiulani and across Kalakaua to the Moana Hotel, then along the beach towards the famous crater. Tourists, servicemen, locals, surfers, beach boys, and beautiful women are on the scene. Old men and beach boys play chess and checkers at the tables in the picnic pavilions near the surfboard rentals.

He takes it all in, goes into a shop, buys new clothes, goes back to his apartment. He looks around, takes off the uniform, stands naked (tanned above the waist, white below) on the lanai. A huge banyan tree shades his end of the courtyard, its population of mynahs in raucous conversation.

In the early evening, he steps out—canvas shoes, loose slacks, and a Hawai'ian shirt. He goes into a place on Kalakaua, takes a stool at the bar, half-jokingly orders sake, and is surprised when he's served a steaming flask of the warm rice wine. Down the bar, a sailor makes a rude comment about a "Jap drink." Lee ignores him, pours, sips, enjoys his sake, remembering a time and a place in the Philippines.

A little later, stepping outside, he is immediately confronted with a beautiful Oriental woman, who accidentally rubs her wrist across his crotch as the sailor from the bar emerges in a belligerent mood behind him. "You're a Jap lover, huh?"

The man is bigger, but Lee is in good shape. He's surprised but not worried as he turns to confront the sailor, while the woman cowers behind him. The man is drunk, talks like he's going to fight, then seems to lose interest and stumbles back into the bar. The woman is gone and so is Lee's wallet.

Leaden haze overcasts the shallow bay of Waikiki. Tantalus has disappeared in cloud. The sea is calm, but it does not rain. A pair of large, brown cockroaches meet, identify one another, and continue on their way.

March of '48, Lee is playing chess at one of the tables with an older Hawai'ian gentleman. A few regulars share the table, playing their own games; others look over shoulders. One big fella, a beach boy named Kimo, is telling Lee what he already knows: "Big waves come in d' summer, y'know, li' dat. What you like take d' car to go surfin' in d' country? You gonna die out there all alone, yeah? Those da kine dumpers! Those other two haoles, they went drown out there in d' winter forty-tree, eh?"

"Just one of 'em died," Lee says, moving his rook. "Check."

"Still all d' same," Kimo rolls on, "that's all blue water out there on d' Haleiwa side. V-e-r-y deep water . . . lots a' current . . . nobody gonna save your haole ass. Better you wait. D' south swells, they be here any time now."

But Lee has his eye on the beautiful woman walking toward him. She's alone, strolling slowly past the pavilions, the breeze rippling a silk mu'u mu'u over her sleek brown body. She appears to be hapa haole, possibly an Oriental mix, and she's smiling, watching all the men playing checkers and chess. Lee feels he's seen her before. When she gets to his table, he engages her in conversation. They seem to recognize each other—there is an exchange of energy. But this is 1948, so they don't acknowledge it.

"You play chess?"

"Me? Oh no. When I was a little girl . . . with my father. But . . . no." Her English is elegant; she is reserved yet assured.

She says her name is Elizabeth, that she's in town to clear up some paperwork with the Department of the Navy. Her husband was a haole, killed in a kamikaze attack at Midway. Recently the government checks stopped coming for no apparent reason. She lives on the Haleiwa side. She's just waiting around for her ride back out to the country . . . she has about an hour to kill.

"I could take you," Lee offers.

"No, thank you."

"Really, it's no problem."

"I don't think so. I have my ride, you see."

"Do you come to town often?"

"Good-bye."

He watches her leaving, feels the theft of her presence.

Green mountains rise to rocky spires that buttress a razor-edged ridgeline. A covey of white birds flashes synchronized figure-eights. The ocean is a very deep blue, spattered with bursts of white.

A few days later, Lee in his new Ford coupe (a redwood/balsa surfboard lashed to the roof) takes the narrow road through Wahiawa and down the great green cane-covered slope to Haleiwa. There's a swell, and the surf is running big . . . whitewater blanketing the offshore reefs of Oahu's North Shore. He drives down into the idyllic sugar plantation town . . . peaceful and beautiful. Few haoles, no tourists. Very slow and tropical.

He drives through town, over the rust-colored bridge and out Kamehameha

Highway, curving around Waimea Bay, to Sunset Beach. He parks and watches the large, powerful waves breaking far from shore.

A car with surfboards on the roof goes past, heading toward town. Curious, Lee jumps in his car and follows. The surfers pull off the highway in Haleiwa and head towards the beach. Lee follows along the cratered dirt road, bouncing out to the beach near a small lava-rock jetty at the mouth of the Anahulu Stream.

Three young men have scrambled out of the car to check the surf. It's good. They unload their boards—strange, streamlined redwood darts with narrow vee-shaped tails. They rub the decks with paraffin wax and charge into the rip. Soon they're streaking across curling ten-foot walls of water. To Lee's eyes, this surfing is so futuristic, it's out of another dimension. This is not how they surf in town.

He watches a long time, then he gets in the car and bounces back to the highway. And then, as he's driving out of Haleiwa, he catches a glimpse of a woman—Elizabeth!—walking near a house on a side street. He brakes, backs up, turns down the street. Small bungalows, shaded from the sun, a few locals, but no sign of her. He drives back and forth, searching. People begin to glare. Reluctantly he gives it up.

A Ford coupe parked on a hot Honolulu side street in the sun. Under the car, spots of black oil shine like coins. The strum of a ukulele.

Next day. Lee enters a nondescript building on a Honolulu side street. Small sign: KGMB RADIO.

Lee is at a microphone. He reads a commercial spot:

"Remember your loved ones back on the mainland with a carton of sweet, delicious Dole Hawai'ian pineapples delivered fresh from the field via air freight—right to their door. Call Aloha 4326 to place your order now."

He segues into a brief weather forecast, which includes a rudimentary surf report—heavy seas in the neighboring channels and strong trade winds.

"The surf is starting to rise today at Waikiki, but if you are touring out on the windward and north side . . . you might just see some waves out there, too . . . "

After that, he puts on a 78 rpm swing record, Count Basie's "One O'clock Jump."

On the way out of the studio Lee throws a few lines at the station manager: "I'm a salesman, I'm a record spinner, I'm a weatherman, and I take calls from goofballs looking for their lost dogs. It's too much, man! How do I tell 'em the dog's not lost, he's a special guest at somebody's dinner?"

The surfboard surges with each powerful stroke of the paddling beach boy. The young lady from Indiana watches the nose of the board shatter spray off the chop. The beach is distant. Diamond Head looms. The surfer is aroused; he caresses the tourist.

Waikiki Beach. There are three surf clubs, the old and moneyed Outrigger Canoe Club, the locals-only Hui O He'e Nalu, and the Waikiki Surf Club, where the California transplants hang out. Lee arrives wearing surf trunks and a T-shirt, which he removes. His surfboard is in the rack, shaded against the side of the building, a few feet from the popular deck of the Waikiki Tavern, where surfers mix with Hollywood celebrities and the daughters of vacationing moguls. This afternoon, a number of women are lounging on the beach between the two buildings, flirting with surfers and beach boys.

A redwood "plank" surfboard—a tourist rental—is laid across a couple of sawhorses. Kimo is patching a bashed-in section of the nose.

"So, Kimo, tell me," says Lee, "did you ever try the waves out Haleiwa side?"

"Sure, alla time when we was kids. Flat alla summer time, then all dumpin' over in d' winter. That's a place to get your surfboard broke, haole boy. Get your head broke, too."

"I saw some guys out there."

"Where?"

"Haleiwa."

"Haleiwa? No way—musta been small . . . that place all bad dumpers—it all comes over, not like this," meaning the beautiful, forgiving Waikiki rollers.

Lee paddles out and joins his friends, gathered together on the fringes of the deeper reefs out toward Diamond Head, waiting to catch waves and ride them on their big, heavy surfboards all the way to the inside seawall.

Duke Kahanamoku is back in town. He's been to Hollywood, where he played a Pacific Islander for the first time, working with John Wayne in a film called *Wake of the Red Witch*. Duke and the Duke. He's sheriff of Honolulu again—part Uncle Tom on the beach, but still the Big Kahuna in the water. Lee asks Duke if he's ever surfed on the North Shore.

"Oh, not fo' long time," says the still-fit, silver-haired Olympic swimming champ. "When I was keiki, I gave it a try, but . . . y'know . . . in th' ol' days, I t'ink they did that—I t'ink they did surf at those places back in those days."

Later, paddling in after a last ride, Lee spots a woman walking away down the beach. Painted gold by the lowering sun, she reminds him of Elizabeth.

He can't tell if it's her. He returns his surfboard to the rack, then hurries back onto the beach to find her. He walks a mile or so but never sees her. The way she has vanished convinces him it was Elizabeth.

Tall glass half-filled with pale gold liquid sweats a widening puddle at its base. A bitten chunk of pineapple, a long wooden toothpick, a wet matchbook. The waitress wipes the table.

The Waikiki Tavern. Between Kalakaua and beach. Step in off the sidewalk, go through the bar and out onto a covered lanai that extends out to the water on pilings that are splashed by the waves at high tide. The bar is open to the evening air. Lee sits at one of a constellation of tables drawn together in a prime spot claimed by the beach boys and some of the surfers. Pioneer surfer Tom Blake is here, feeling uncomfortable in the social setting. He is on his annual sojourn to the Islands, but he's been threatening never to return—too many tourists.

Another area of the bar is occupied with a few sophisticated Asians, possibly white slavers or smugglers, although there is nothing sophisticated about the Waikiki Tavern. A big Hawai'ian man at a far table watches Lee intently.

Later, at the radio station, a 78 record spins—Frank Sinatra, "How Deep Is the Ocean." As it ends, Lee announces an upcoming interclub paddling race at Waikiki.

"Be sure to come by Waikiki Beach this Saturday for the big paddle race. Maybe, if we're lucky, there'll be some of those bluebirds to ride."

On the beach a few days later, it's Eddie Moepono vs. Bobby Carter. Big Eddie is the paddling king of Waikiki. Bobby is younger and smaller, but an experienced street fighter. This is a big showdown. They race just off the beach, a sprint from the Outrigger Canoe Club out around a pair of buoys and into the beach in front of the Waikiki Tavern. When Bobby wins going away, Big Eddie complains that Bobby's board is faster. So they switch boards, and Bobby wins again—by more distance. Big Eddie is taciturn, not happy. Bobby is elated, but humble.

Carter is one of a tight group of younger surfers that ride a different style of surfboard—the streamlined boards Lee saw at Haleiwa. He realizes now that Bobby was one of those guys.

High in a coco palm, among nuts and berries, a rat pauses, sniffs the air. An airplane soars northward, disappearing over Tantalus. Footsteps passing on the sidewalk below—a uniformed man, delivering the mail.

A fenced backyard in the Waikiki backstreets—the rasping sound of a hand-plane working away on balsa wood. Californian Joe Quigg is shaping a new Malibu-style surfboard behind a house rented by mainlanders Dave Benson and Steve Kaplan. Quigg is something of a celebrity, so Bobby Carter is there, along with a young, heavy-set beach boy named Luau Boy. Lee shows up with a carton of Primo beer. "Looks like a smoker," he offers the taciturn Quigg. "It's a *stoker*," says Quigg without looking up, "no doubt about it."

The balsa board is a cross between the standard boxy redwood planks and the streamlined darts they call hot-curl boards. But this balsa board has hydrodynamic rails, exotic bottom contours, a narrow pointed stern Quigg calls a "pintail," and a wooden fin that's shaped like a shark's.

Later, Quigg seals the board with a layer of fiberglass cloth painted with resin. When it hardens, the new surfboard is buffed to a gloss; the world is all new and different, strangely revealed.

Lee wants one of these surfboards to ride at Waikiki, but Luau Boy snorts his disapproval. "Those old beach boys are fat and lazy, and so are d' waves here. We go out to d' country to surf these t'ings—Maile and Makaha—plenty waves over that side."

Fields of cane bending to the trades, a red dirt road slashing through, rising up green slopes toward the Waianae range. An opaque puddle gleams with blue sky as a foot-long centipede drinks.

On the road to Makaha, Carter, Kaplan, Benson, and Lee in Kaplan's Model A, boards piled on wooden roof racks. Past Ewa Beach there are beautiful transparent turquoise waves at Maile. The road is paved but minimal out to the turnoff for Kolekole Pass, then it's dirt. They pass the M. Ni'i store in Waianae, where the surfers have their trunks made by the little Japanese tailor.

The surf at Makaha is not as big as the local Hawai'ians who check out the haoles. The one called Columbus wants to know who Lee is. Luau Boy makes the introduction, and then it's okay. The surf is small and looks fun; the wind is offshore, as usual. The waves are beautiful and perfect, and the guys paddle out, Lee on his new Quigg surfboard. It's a revelation—loose, light, and maneuverable.

The waves are breaking on the inside at Makaha, peeling over the lime-green moss of the reef like a paradisiacal Malibu. Luau Boy is a master of hot-curl surfing, riding his red torpedo across the transparent late-afternoon waves with all the poise and eloquence of a great dancer.

Waiting for a set as the sun is lowering on a clear horizon, Carter directs Lee's attention towards land's end, a few miles north. "Kaena Point," he nods. "In the winter, when it gets really big here, it gets really, really big out there. We go check it out some time come then, eh." It was not a question.

Water-stained and yellowed newspapers cover the wall. Cans of pork and beans crowd a solitary wood shelf. A fat yellow cane spider waits in a web outside a small, dirty window. Beyond, dark clouds crowd the peaks.

Winter 1950. The sun slants down the throat of Makaha Valley, where Steve Kaplan and Mack Irons, an ex-Marine from California, have rented a quonset hut (one of several in the area abandoned by the military) just across from the golden sands of Makaha. Increasing numbers of itinerant Californians—big-wave pioneers—are hanging around. Lee has his own "weekend" bunk in the shack, and a U.S. Army pennant hangs over the narrow, plank bed. Out in the yard a surfboard-building operation has been set up to supply the community's equipment needs.

On this day, Makaha Point is flat. Lee wants to drive over to the Haleiwa side, but no one else shares his enthusiasm. He doesn't have a permit to go over Kolekole Pass, so he decides to try the drive around Kaena Point, his surfboard strapped to the top of the Ford.

Out past Makaha, the road deteriorates from dirt to mud to giant puddles to a narrow rocky traverse. A couple of times he has to stop and find driftwood, rocks, and pieces of ubiquitous corrugated metal siding to build a ramp so he can drive over bouldered or cratered sections of the path. At last he arrives at the lighthouse, an unmanned white tower, anchored on a barren finger of land which boldly juts northwest out into the Pacific—Kaena Point. Today, the ocean appears blue, sparkling, and serene—like a calm day in Southern California. But when a solitary wave steepens, darkens, and peels, it gives Lee a hint of what will come with the giant winter storms.

The road from the lighthouse along the north coast to Haleiwa is better-maintained; it curves around beautiful coves and along exquisite beaches. A mile or so before Mokuleia, Lee spots a perfect sandy cove. He pulls over to the side of the road and looks out. A bicycle leans against a kiawe tree near where a woman swims alone in a perfect warm-water pool. He gets out of the car, walks down. Her hair has been cut short, and her body is paler than he remembers, but it is undoubtedly Elizabeth.

"Hello!" he calls and waves. She turns and looks up at him, startled.

He takes off his hat. "Remember me?"

She doesn't appear to recognize him at all. She looks around, slightly alarmed to find herself alone in a remote place with a strange man.

"Did you sort out that business with the government checks?" he asks, moving closer. She doesn't seem to know what he's talking about. "Your husband . . . killed in the war."

What husband? What war? She says she is a Zen Buddhist. Her name is Midori. "I have never been married," she says.

Lee feels momentarily disoriented. Could he be mistaken? He redirects the conversation to the moment.

"Well," he blushes, "you really look like someone I met in town. I mean, almost exactly."

She finds his obvious embarrassment disarming.

"Wow," he exhales. "It's hot. Mind if I join you?" She makes an acquiescent gesture, and he joins her in the water.

They swim. He is explosively attracted to her, almost can't bear it. Too soon, she leaves the water. He offers her a ride home, but she refuses and packs her things into a basket. He pretends to check his tires as she mounts her bike and pedals off towards Haleiwa; after a few minutes, he gets in and follows at a short distance, watching her body move in the saddle. He pounds the steering wheel and screams with frustration, struggling with her contradictory story.

At Mokuleia, Lee drives past her, waving, and heads towards Haleiwa. Just before the Waialua bridge, he pulls off into a cane field near the sugar mill and waits for her to pass, but she never does.

Buzzing fly bounces across bright window. Somewhere a radio plays "Somewhere There's Music" by Les Paul and Mary Ford. Telex softly clatters across yellow paper. A transmission from a freighter warns of heavy seas to the north. The ship has suffered damage off French Frigate Shoals and is heading into port.

Lee calls Carter from the radio station with the news. The moment his shift is over, he blasts out to Makaha. There, he and the other guys gather in the ochre dusk to watch tiny waves slapping serenely onto the shore.

They sit around a campfire, drink and talk. Lee brings up the meeting with Elizabeth, or Midori—whoever she is. Carter advises him that there are great mysteries in the universe, and one mystery every real surfer learns well is that you can't catch a wave unless you're in the right place at precisely the right time. "It's d' same with every t'ing," he says.

During the night, Lee is awakened by a rumbling vibration in the earth. He slips out of bed and leaves the hut, heads across the road and walks out to the point at Makaha. Carter and Irons are already there. The air is filled with a heavy mist of salt spray and the roar of waves. Their huge black shapes rise and smoke in the moonlight.

At dawn the surfers are on the beach, waxing their boards. The surf is huge. "You comin'?" asks Carter. "Dunno," says Lee. Irons, the ex-Marine (roasting the enemy with a flamethrower while Lee was operating a radio), goads him on, virtually commanding Lee to confront the challenge at hand.

"Come on, Sizemore! This is the moment you were born for—this is life! No time to shirk. Muster your mettle. Let's go!"

Carter attempts to soften things. "You'll know when you're ready, yeah?" he says, patting Lee's shoulder. "Mack's got no sense sometimes."

But Irons prevails, and Lee paddles out. If the situation with Elizabeth-Midori is surreal, this is beyond surreal. The waves are like God's special effects—dark blue walls of water that wedge high above them and are always fringing out beyond Lee, so that he's continually clawing for survival, barely paddling over the sets. Meanwhile, Carter and Irons are in ecstasy, blazing trails through the thundering hollows of these powerful giants spawned thousands of miles to the north in an Aleutian storm.

Finally, a peak shifts and lifts right outside of Lee. With a groan of decision, he turns his board around and makes a committed effort to paddle into it. Suddenly he hurtles forward and starts the chattering descent. He makes it to the bottom and carves a cautious turn as the top of the wave throws out over his head and explodes in front of him, cutting off his escape. It's a bad wipeout. He scratches to the surface—his board is gone and another wave is about to break on him. When he surfaces again, he is in the river of rip current sweeping down the coast past Klausmeyer's house, then out towards Japan. "Oh, great," he mutters to himself, suppressing a chill of panic.

He is astonished how swiftly the current is moving him down the coast and away from the beach. Staying afloat but increasingly hopeless in the heaving chop of the rip, Lee is startled to hear a voice close at hand. "Hey, haole, you like help?" It's Columbus on a big tandem board come out to rescue him. "I almos' din't nevah see you out 'ere. Mo' betta you watch from d' beach, eh?"

Out in the surf, Carter and Irons watch a wave approach. Carter says, "Take it." Irons says, "I got it," and Carter watches him drop down the sheer face. But when Carter turns to look back out to sea, he has to rub his eyes to confirm what he's seeing: up the coast towards Kaena Point, the horizon is a dark black line. At first it seems to be shadow, but there are no clouds.

Realizing a monster is approaching, Carter lies on his board and puts his paddling prowess to work, stroking steadily out to sea. When he looks back towards the beach, the cars parked on the road are unidentifiable specs. Ahead of him, the first wave of the set is arriving—a 40-foot wall of water with whitewater boiling off of its crest. Paddling up it is like paddling up and over a mountain cornice.

The next wave is steeper, like paddling up the face of a building. To Carter's right, an immense curl folds over to form a tube big enough to surround a two-story house. Still he paddles out, though his arms and lungs are on fire, until he crests the next wave—pushing through the smoking crest to find the outside wave bigger still and already cascading over at the top.

Carter takes several huge breaths and holds the last as he shoves his surf-board aside and dives into the face of the mountain. Immediately he is under forty feet of water, and the sudden pressure bursts his eardrums. He claws towards the bottom, then turns to watch the concussion of the wave as it bursts into a submarine boil, sending large boulders bouncing around like pebbles. The dull, thudding sounds are terrifying.

Fearing another monster is about to break, Carter gingerly crawls back up to the surface, only to find a flat horizon and a thick layer of spent foam dissolving with a hissing sound in the warm morning sun. Oozing blood from his nose and ears, he begins the slow, painful swim for shore.

Old Hawai'ian woman sits on the porch of a palm-sheltered windward Oahu cottage listening to radio news—cease-fire in Korea. Bright sun darkens to huge downpour as a man on a bicycle pedals past.

In 1953, mad scientist Bob Simmons is pedaling his bike (surfboard in tow) along the north coast of the island. He stops at Ehukai Beach and watches perfect waves curl over, makes an entry in his notebook, damaged left elbow jutting out, then pedals on. Just before the bridge in Haleiwa, having developed quite a thirst, he pulls over and leans his bike against the side of the Sands, a rather shabby restaurant and bar.

Though it is afternoon, it might as well be midnight in the bar. A couple of locals sitting on stools give Simmons the evil eye, but he appears oblivious. He asks the bartender if he has wheat grass juice or some equally bolstering natural tonic.

"How 'bout a beer?"

"Nope," Simmons pronounces. "Gotta be nonalcoholic. How 'bout papaya or pineapple juice?"

The bartender pours a glass of milk and sticks it in front of Simmons. It's curdled and sour. Simmons drinks it.

"Ah!" he says, savoring the putrid liquid. "Thanks." He makes a couple of unappreciated observations on the intestinal benefits of certain bacilli.

The two big Hawai'ians at the pool table, already perturbed that this unknown haole has entered their inner sanctum, are in no mood to listen. They decide they're "gonna broke his head." But as they start to press their mission, the door swings in and the whole Makaha crew tumbles into the bar, among them Mack, Lee, and Columbus.

Quickly reading the situation as his eyes adjust to the darkness, Mack steps in front of the locals.

"C'mon, boys, leave the little guy alone, will ya?"

One of the Hawai'ians snorts—not a chance!—and a classic bar fight ensues. Uncharacteristically, Columbus abstains, being in some confusion over which side he should be on. The mixer is quelled when he takes a ukulele from the wall and begins singing—in a surprisingly beautiful voice—a Hawai'ian song of friendship.

They all end up getting drunk and singing together. They learn that Bob Simmons has come here from California to map the island's reefs for big-wave surfing—and to try out some new ideas he has developed around his prototype foam-filled surfboards. He wants to build a surfboard specifically designed for very large surf. He is especially interested in the waves off Kaena Point.

Old Hawai'ian man poles a small, flat-bottomed skiff across smooth red water through a forest of mango and hau trees. Rusted steel bridge arcs above. Ahead, the stream opens out to the ocean, surf bursting over reef.

Lee drives into Haleiwa, parks his car at the beach and gets out. Elizabeth (or is it Midori?) sits on the grassy berm at the edge of the sand, wearing a print dress and a sun hat, watching the waves. He sits near her, but she ignores him. She seems almost entranced.

"Hello again," he says, but she doesn't answer. He follows her gaze, out towards the horizon. "What are you looking at?"

"Nothing," she answers in a low voice, almost a whisper.

"I see," he answers. "What's your name today?"

She says her name is Nani, that she's looking for the sails of her father's great voyaging canoe. A faithful reconstruction of an ancient vessel. He built it single-handedly, the work of a lifetime. Now in his seventies, he took the boat on its maiden voyage, to Niihau, ten days ago—from here, from Haleiwa harbor—and his return is several days overdue.

"Do you remember me?" he asks. She seems surprised at the question, shakes her head "no."

"I'm Lee. I work at the radio station? KGMB in Honolulu? I spin records, and I surf. We met at Waikiki, and out by Kaena Point . . . swimming?"

She levels a look at him and slowly shakes her head. "No."

Lee is mystified. She's as beautiful as she was the first time he saw her, but the intensity of his attraction is leavened with the creeping suspicion that she's crazy—a person with multiple personalities perhaps?

Just then a black panel truck lurches up to the beach. It's Carter and Irons checking the surf. They notice Lee and come over, wising off, sharing small talk.

"I think he will not come today," says the woman, meaning her voyaging father. Then she rises abruptly and excuses herself with a slight, distinctly formal bow. The surfers watch her leave without comment.

"Somethin' ya said?" says Mack with a mocking tone.

Lee ignores him, gets up and follows her. She walks out the dirt road, weaving uncertainly around the deep ruts filled with the mud-red water. When she looks back over her shoulder, Lee averts his gaze and walks purposefully off towards a run-down bungalow. Then he turns back onto the road and continues to follow, and she doesn't look back again. She walks to the street where Lee thought he'd seen her five years earlier and disappears around the side of the same house.

After a few seconds, he follows—around the house, across a lawn, around a small garage, through a cluster of mature mango trees, and into a strange and exotic garden of ferns, flowers, and found objects. She (whatever her name) is disappearing up a rustic spiral of wooden stairs winding around the trunk of a large banyan, leading up to a kind of treehouse suspended in its arms. He decides to follow . . .

He's pulled back abruptly, dragged out of the grove, and thrown hard against the garage wall. Two large Oriental men confront him. "Where you think you go, huh?" says the older one. "You wish to die or what?" asks the other.

They drag Lee out to the road and shove him sprawling into a puddle of red water as Bobby and Mack approach. "Keep this haole asshole away from our sister or we cut his balls off." Lee scrambles to his feet and staggers out of the puddle towards his friends.

"You got the message?" asks the younger guy. Lee nods, backing away. The surfers return to their cars, glancing back over their shoulders.

"Scary guys," says Lee. Bobby nods.

"Cute girl," says Mack.

Steamship horn blasts, bouncing off downtown buildings. Sailors in white bell-bottoms stroll Hotel Street, chewing gum and smoking, casually laughing, their faces red, their eyes on the move.

A few days later, Lee's at the radio station, playing Johnny Ray, when the phone rings through to him.

"Is this Lee?" He recognizes her voice immediately.

"Yes, hello. Who is this?"

"Nani. From Haleiwa. You told me where you work. Can you help me?" She says she's at a pay phone and only has a minute to talk. She's being held against her will, a prisoner of those thugs, those gangsters. It started with stolen Red Cross morphine after the war. She had been a hospital administrator; she'd helped them. Don't ask why. But when the booty ran out, they had hundreds of customers, so they made the move to a more commercial venture, trafficking opium and heroin from Southeast Asia.

"Do you believe me?" she asks.

"How can I?" he says.

"But this is the truth," she says. "You must believe me." He doesn't answer. "You don't believe me?"

"No," he says. "I don't know."

"I will prove it to you," she says. "I will meet you."

"Where?"

There is a pause. "The lighthouse. Tomorrow, after midnight . . . at Kaena Point."

Pockets of mist hang low in each small dip of the road. The Waianae ridgeline silhouetted black against the dawn. Rooster scratches the cool earth, bristles his neck feathers, startles himself with his own crow.

The quonset hut at Makaha. Simmons lies on one of the beds reading a newspaper. Bobby and Mack are eating canned beans and rice. Lee is nervous. His last encounter with the woman frightened him—not only because of the two thugs, but because of her apparent schizophrenia. Her story seems to go a long way towards explaining things, however, and this inclines him to follow through with a meeting. Bobby disagrees.

"Hey, look," he says, "it's like 'dis—you t'inking with your head or with your dick? Only you can say f' sure. But you gotta use you' head on dis one, eh?"

Lee appreciates his counsel but already knows the answer. He looks out the cabin window, up the valley. Straight over that ridge is Haleiwa.

"She's beautiful, huh?" he says.

Mack lets out a "Shit!" of disgust and goes outside. The sound of a rasp across balsa begins immediately. Lee shrugs.

Simmons looks up from the paper, considers, then volunteers. "I'll go with you."

"Really?" says Lee. Simmons nods, looks back at the paper. "Thanks."

"Ship transmissions from the north are talking about very large swells," says Simmons. "I'd really like to see that before I go back to California."

Gecko on fence post, one eye on moon. Palms rattle and sway. Distant rumbling, rushing sounds closer. A great surge of whitewater sweeps up from the beach, surrounds a cottage, carries off toys, lanai furniture, a small dog.

The midnight hour. Lee's coupe bounces and rocks out the cratered road toward Kaena Point, surfboards are strapped to the roof, shifting around, almost coming off. Somewhere off to the left, huge waves are breaking. Great masses of whitewater rush the rugged shore, lunge up the low cliffs and drown the road. The car pauses frequently to let the torrent of saltwater and mud subside before crossing low spots on the narrow track.

Inside the car, Simmons appears oblivious, regaling, technologizing, predicting, swearing. "There is absolutely no reason why you couldn't ride a hundred-foot wave—if you got your planing surface, which is your greatest source of friction, down to a small enough factor, and if you could acquire sufficient paddling speed to catch the damn thing, because these huge ocean swells are traveling one helluva lot faster than your typical surfing waves. But, say you could get towed into one of these monsters by a boat—like a water-skier—that could work!"

Lee grips the steering wheel and strains to see the road ahead as the wipers streak the steady mist of gritty saltwater spray across the windshield. The headlights are dim, and the going is treacherous. He is not listening. The road and the woman fully occupy his thoughts.

Finally, reaching a wet ramp of corrugated metal laid over the rocks at the final rise, Lee stops the car and switches off the headlights.

"Never make it up this part," he says. "It's not far. I can walk."

Simmons peers out into the blackness. "Uh-huh."

"If something happens . . . if I don't come back—call the cops."

"Uh-huh."

As the door slams, Simmons slides across to the driver's seat and rolls down the window. He watches Lee scramble up the rocky slope and disappear into the night. He takes a deep breath of warm, saturated air and sighs, listening to the thunder of the surf, trying to see something.

Sound of surf. Moon riding high in the sky. A large glass lens plate snaps closed, a switch snaps, an explosion of light. The sound of footsteps on a metal ladder, then a car starts and drives off. The lighthouse beacon is flashing . . . turning . . . flashing . . .

It's the middle of the night, and spray fills the air like a salty smoke. The trail up the point is treacherous—bouldered and slick and dark. Lee is disoriented until he spots the lighthouse ahead, standing perilously close to the raging ocean. The beacon is dark, the white tower illuminated only by the dim moon above. Then, further on, coming up out of a dip in the road, the beacon is lit and turning, and his skin crawls briefly as he suffers a brief wave of dread.

As the beacon sweeps its arc, Lee can see big waves erupting on the reefs far out to sea as he follows the path to the lighthouse. Almost there, he stops and stares down the road toward Haleiwa and seems to see a lone figure walking. He starts to call out, but a sudden jab to his throat chokes him silent. The two thugs are there. As Lee gags for breath, Kimo steps into view.

"What you t'inkin', haole?" Kimo looks back at the departing figure. "I tol' you not t' go country, eh?" When he again turns to Lee, his fist immediately follows.

Low in the dark bush, wild pig trotting along familiar trail, head turning side to side, tusks sometimes snagging branches, snorting, searching, panting. Left turn, right turn, left turn, right turn. In the bright sky above, an iwa bird soars, motionless on the wind.

Lee opens his eyes to pain. Surprised by the gray light of dawn, he finds himself sitting at the base of the lighthouse. He can dimly make out the road to Haleiwa . . . deserted.

He struggles to his feet, notices the blood spattered around, gingerly explores his face and head—multiple contusions and abrasions. Lots of tender spots, and his nose is broken. He's glad he wasn't around for it.

He staggers around the lighthouse to discover magnificent waves marching in from the northwest. A giant smoking swell peaks and peels off toward the end of Kaena Point—an incredible monster with a wall that seems to go all the way to Japan. And sliding along the wall, caught briefly in the silvery light of the beacon, is a surfer. Simmons!

A great, green surge heaves against the jagged shore, burrows relentlessly into seams and pits and holes, and drives up through an ancient lava tube, exploding out into a great geyser of white spray. In the tumult, small black crabs scramble, preparing for the next wave.

Simmons won't shut up, but Lee isn't listening.

"Amazing thing . . . it's all in the book. It's written down. You've just gotta do it. It's physics. Physics is physics, and a law's a law, 'cuz you can't break it. Can't bend it neither. If you could, it wouldn't be a law. Flat means no drag. Slightest curve, that equals drag. Water ain't compressible. It's soooo basic . . . "

Lee carefully nurses the Ford over rocks and slick red pieces of corrugated metal and across a narrow isthmus in the road as Simmons leans out the window for one last look back at the waves. His back, still beaded with saltwater, is streaked with cuts and bleeding.

Lee looks over. "I can't believe you survived that."

"Yeah."

Lee snorts, glances up into the mirror, meets her eyes . . . like chocolate stones. Skin like . . .

He feels her cool fingertips on the side of his neck, puts his own hand over them, wonders who she is.

This story is previously unpublished.

the lost coast

IT WAS WEDNESDAY, a bad day in the middle of a bad week just about dead center in a bad winter, and I was running a bad stretch of cabin fever. It'd been raining for three months, a few sun breaks short of nonstop. They don't call it the Pacific Northwet for nothing. Out the window, the slow-motion surf plowing up the strait was huge but junk. A couple of Indians were having trouble getting their aluminum boat back in through the waves with their early morning salmon catch. I half-filled a mug of coffee, dumped in two glugs of Jack Daniels, and went back upstairs to check the e-mail. I had deadlines, but I was having trouble getting to the point, if you know what I mean.

There were five messages; one was interesting, and timely. It was from the editor of *Hotdogger* magazine. Here's what it said:

To: Zeke Austen <tubular@pacrim.com>
Subject: a story???
Date: Tue, 10 Feb 1999 10:44:36 -0800
Zeke,

I've got a strange proposal: A few months ago we received a thick manila envelope stuffed with surf photos—35mm slides in plastic sleeves, 23 sleeves, 20 slides each (except one sheet had one slide missing, and it wasn't in the envelope), so 459 shots all told. But: no return address on the envelope, no I.D. on the slides, totally unmarked, unlabeled, even unnumbered and undated plastic slide mounts. There are 3 or 4 surfers in the pics, but no one here at the mag recognizes them. And the shots are good—very, very good.

Flame thought they looked like NorCal, so he called Vince Lyons, who used to fish that part of the coast before he got involved with Surfrider and moved down here. So Vince came in and had a look, and he recognized the headland and setup in

some of the shots. He says they were taken near the rivermouth between Punta
Gorda and Cape Mendocino. He can't believe anyone would surf there—it's the
sharkiest place on the entire Pacific coast—but he swears that's the place.

Your assignment, should you choose to accept it . . .

I didn't have to read the rest. The day had gone from bad to worse. I'd queried
the magazine on covering the Noosa longboard thing, the ASP event in Tavarua,
and the expatriate scene in Biarritz, and this is what they come up with—playing
main course on the buffet in some NorCal hell's kitchen, and all for a few pieces
of silver. I didn't especially need the money, but I needed a break in the weather,
badly. Like most people up here, I'm subject to seasonal affective disorder; about
February, I get cranky and feel like killing people, starting with myself.

It rained all the way to Coos Bay, and then it got worse. The lineup at Hubbard
Creek looked like whipped chocolate with log cabins floating around in it like
marshmallows. At Gold Beach, I saw trucks washing out under the bridge; the
waves were breaking out so far they re-formed twice before they slammed into
the driftwood-lined beach. By the time I crossed the border and made my way
down to Crescent City, the wipers on my Isuzu Trooper were shredded and
flailed at the windshield like dreadlocks. I was bumming till I scored in Arcata
and slipped a Tuff Gong CD into the slot, oh yeah.

The sun came out just south of Eureka; I put on my sunglasses and went
back to track 1. Everything was fine till I got to Fortuna. Something about the
way the sign looked back at me—FORTUNA—made me consider.

Fortuna. Fortune. Fate.

Fortuna. Fortune. Wealth.

Fortuna. For tuna. As in, "Great whites looking for tuna." I pulled in and
got gas and studied my Thomas Brothers map book.

They call the stretch of coast south of Eureka "the Lost Coast" for a lot of reasons, but I wasn't sure I wanted to know them all. The fact that you couldn't get
there from here was one thing. The whole place was rugged, treacherous, and
unstable, and Highway 101 swung inland for almost seventy-five miles to bypass
the whole mess. Most all the land west of the road was primitive State land.

The river I was after swept into the Pacific at the most remote spot on the coast. An old Victorian mansion, built by Sebastian de Miranda in the late nineteenth century, is the only residence on the entire coast, with the exception of the notorious Blackthorn compound at Big Flat, over twenty miles to the south. No question about it, the place was remote.

I didn't have to be told about the sharks either. I knew plenty. A friend of mine works out of the little harbor at Trinidad; a couple years ago, he and his fishing buddy were coming back north loaded to the gunnels with halibut. When the boat rounded Punta Gorda, it was attacked by several huge great whites, and his friend lost part of a hand. They were pitching whole halibut off the stern to buy off The Landlord when one came over the transom and snagged a hundred-pounder right out of his arms.

I tried not to think about it as I swung off Highway 101 and scouted out a market. I figured I needed three days, so I bought grub for five. I planned to park at the beach, sleep in the back with my surfboards, but I'd have to find somebody I could convince to get me through the gate to the Miranda estate. I knew (from my Trinidad friend) that the old Miranda house was now owned and maintained by the State of California; it wasn't open to the public, but you could walk into the beach if you were up to a refreshing fifteen-mile hike. I'd rather my tires did the walking.

As it turned out, the Miranda gate was buttoned up tight, and even a 50-mph charge into it with my 'roo bar wouldn't have changed that, so I began to troll for back roads indicated in my map book by parallel broken lines. I was scraping along between dense manzanita on one of these tracks about seven miles south of the gate when a break in the action passed by on the right. I put it into reverse and had a look. It was a narrow cattle gate—wired shut but unlocked—with a battered and rusting sign screwed into the top bar. It said: TRESPASSERS WILL BE EATEN! and there were the silhouettes of two sharks. This was encouraging.

I unraveled the wire, opened the gate, and pulled in a couple hundred feet. Then I went back, tore a branch off a bush, swept my turn-off tracks away, and cleared my traces back to the car. I stood and surveyed the situation. I was in a recently logged swale; it was warm—in fact, the sun was hot here—and the only sound was the hum of insects punctuated by the occasional z-z-z-Z-Z-Z-z-z-z of a passing bumblebee. Three black turkey vultures circled lazily, high in the acid blue sky. Mountains blocked the south and west and north, and the road forked just ahead.

I opened the book on the hood of the car and found where I thought I was, but this little bit of dirt road didn't make the map. I figured I could take the left fork, but it might not go over the mountains, and if it did, it might end up on the south side of the river, which came down out of the western slopes angling towards the north. The road into the house from the main gate was off to the north those seven miles, and I'd likely hit it on the right fork. I'd probably have less chance of being spotted going left, but the road to the house was more of a sure thing. I got back in the car, rolled a fattie, slipped Yo Yo Ma's Bach partitas into the slot, and faded right.

It was a weird, bad place for a gate. I had been heading up a steep, raw cut of road with a sheer drop-off on my right and a wall of loose dirt and rock on my left. I was in four-wheel drive, taking it slow, my tires slipping every time I jumped one of the sharp, softball-sized rocks that littered the narrow track. I was already sweating bullets when I came around a sharp blind curve where the road steepened even more, and right there was the gate. I almost lost my lunch, but I hadn't eaten. I hit the brakes, the Trooper stopped, then slid backwards a few inches before it stopped again. I was very aware of my weight pressing back in the seat, the weight of the car pressing back towards the abyss.

Slowly, carefully, I got out. Slipping in the loose dirt and stone at the side of the road, I felt nauseous when I realized how steep the grade was. I walked down behind the car and wedged a rock behind each tire. The road was so narrow, I couldn't walk around the other side of the car, where the edge dropped straight off, and it was hundreds of feet down. The slope was littered with scree and scattered with brave conifers that rose straight up with their shoulders against the wall. A litter of objects was clustered against the denser edge of forest far below, and the sun glinted off—I guessed—pieces of chrome and glass. I was not amused.

I walked back around the car and up to the gate; it was like climbing stairs. Same kind of gate as the other with a sign that read, TRESPASSERS GO BACK! But there was no going back from here, and it was at that moment that I felt profound love for the salesman who had talked me into adding another $1,388 to the purchase price of the vehicle to install a power winch to the front end. Luckily, there was no lock on this gate either, just wire, but as I was unwrapping it, one nasty, sharp end suddenly twisted and punched deep into the pad below my right thumb. Not good.

The gate wouldn't swing downhill; it was blocked by a post, and it wouldn't stay open in the uphill direction due to the angle of the roadway. I had to collect rocks to pile against the gate, but most of the rocks in the area were small — as I said, softball-sized — and it took me a while to collect them, branding them with blood from my hand. But when I pushed the gate up off to the side and piled the rocks in front of it, the gate swung easily down through the pile, scattering stones down the road. I felt a new surge of panic, but then I slapped myself in the head. Of course! I could hold the gate open with the jack. But the jack handle was too short and too light; it didn't work, and I threw it into the back of the car with a desperate sound that embarrassed me. "Keep it together, you idiot!" I commanded myself.

I thought of the spare tire — maybe I could wedge it in under the gate, maybe . . . and that's when I slapped my head a second time and pulled one of my boards out of the back. I left it in its travel bag to save the nose, which I planted in a run-off groove at the edge of the road, then slipped the middle rail of the gate between the tail and trailing fin of the board, and it held.

I started the car, played out the cable, looped it around the inside post, and slipped the hook back over the cable. This would get me up to the gate where the grade was not as steep. I got back in the car, put it in gear, hit the winch switch and the gas, and it worked: I moved forward smoothly with decent traction, shooting a few rocks off into the abyss, until I got my rear tires into a flatter area near the gate, then I reversed the winch, took it off the post and rewound the cable. Now I was on my own.

I babied the clutch and managed to nudge the Trooper into motion. As it began to climb faster, the tires got better purchase, so rather than stop to close the gate, I kept climbing. Within a mile the track began to level out; the cliff to the left became a rise studded with Douglas fir and alder, and the abyss to the right didn't scare me so much. When I reached a good comfort level I stopped the car, pulled on the emergency brake, left it in gear, and shut off the engine. There were thick clouds of coastal fog up ahead, backlit at the edges with golds and purples by the lowering sun. "That's probably the crest," I thought. I had an old T-shirt under the seat, and I tore off a piece and tied up my right hand, using my teeth and left hand to tighten the knot. Then, just to be safe, I took the keys out of the ignition, locked the car, and headed back down to get my board and close the gate.

But the gate was closed, and my board was gone. Apparently, it had slipped in the loose dirt and the gate had swung closed, but as I held onto the outside post and looked over the edge (feeling that electric quease in my gut), there was no sign of the silver bag, which was strange, because the board was light and large—an 8-footer—and I doubted it could have gone all the way to the bottom. It should have caught on the scree or one of the trees below, but there was no sign of it. Then I went over to secure the gate, and I found the stiff wire wrapped around the post, just the way I'd found it.

"That's one big item for the expense account," I figured as I slogged back to the car in deepening shadow. It was cooling off rapidly on the east side of the mountain, and I was looking forward to a little colorized sunset at the top of the hill. Instead, I found myself walking up through denser and denser mist. I was worried, but I knew as long as I stayed to the left side of the road I couldn't fall or get lost. In the end, I didn't so much find the car as walk into it.

I started the car and continued up the road for another ten or fifteen minutes—maybe a couple of miles—driving slowly in the fog, which was so thick it reminded me of Santa Cruz in June. Finally I came to a wide, flat place, and I lost the road. I stopped and popped a Doors CD into the player and turned it up loud and left the door of the car open while I looked around. It was a crossroads, I determined, then decided that straight ahead was my best bet. "Riders on the Storm" led me back to the car; I couldn't see a thing.

The life of a surf journalist is not a cakewalk, I can tell you. The next three hours were spent in a steep, creeping, switchback descent through darkness, fog, and dripping rainforest. Huge ferns arched out over the car and dragged along the side windows as the wheels humped over roots and boulders and the track went from loose dirt to slick mud. It was almost midnight when the road started to level out, and I came to the third gate. This time the sign said, TRESPASSERS ARE FOOLS! I had to agree.

The gate was padlocked this time—three big ones on three fat chains—but I had lost all patience. I looked over my shoulder and backed up the Trooper a hundred feet or so. When I turned around, the gate had disappeared into the fog. I hit the gas and popped the clutch and put those four little Japanese cylinders to work. I roared up to the gate and . . . it was open! Astonished, I roared through the opening, catching the sign out of the corner of my eye—TRESPASSERS ARE . . . then I slammed on the brakes as a huge black object loomed up out of the foggy night, and the car skidded to a stop in front of a very large Victorian house.

I could hear the thunder of the surf coming through the fog, but no other sound, except the house. The house itself exuded darkness like a roar, like being deep under a ten-meter outer-reef wave that you hoped wasn't going to worm down far enough to suck you up off the bottom and into its terrible vortex. The twin cones of headlight seemed to fade a few inches from the skin of the house—the old redwood clapboards were molded to the frame quite like skin after a hundred-some years in the elements—as if the light were being absorbed into the ancient wood like water into a sponge. I climbed five stairs to the covered veranda and stepped closer. There was one of those signs on the big, filthy front door: TRES-PASSERS KEEP OUT!

I tried the old-fashioned latch and was relieved that it was frozen or locked, I couldn't tell which.

I spent the night right there in my car, doors locked, windows opened an eighth of an inch all round, which gave a nice, cool breeze and let in the low moan of the sea. Still, my sleep was fitful, and I dreamt the kind of dreams you might expect a surf journalist trespasser at a haunted house to dream.

There was a tapping, a tap-tap-tapping, then a scratching and a kind of twisting, and then a breathing—deep and never stopping, the lungs swelling, swelling until the ribs were bowed out like the stretched seams of a dream that burst . . . and I awoke, frantically exhaling that real or imagined breath to see the shape of the car's windows adrift in a void. No sound at all, the surf vanished, the dream scattering off the floor of my consciousness like surprised cockroaches, leaving no trace . . . but a definite feeling. And, yeah, I thought, I need a vacation. I need to get away.

I opened the door and stepped out into the fog. White dust puffed out from under a thin crust of damp as I walked past the house towards the sound that had been there last night. The fog was dazzling and thick. I could see maybe a hundred feet around me as I walked around the right side of the house, following the road along the edge of the yard, which was a study in native grasses and wild-flowers, perfectly ordered with no sign of a human hand. After the dust of the road turned to sand and I walked up a low rise, I could hear the waves again, and when I crested the berm of the beach I saw the most amazing sight.

The fog was lifted out over the water—maybe fifty or a hundred feet of

ceiling—and the sun was shining maybe a mile or so off shore. The ocean out
there was brilliant blue and spattered with bits of whitewater. In closer, under the
shadow of the fog cloud, it was clear but dark, and I saw the rivermouth by a heap
of beached wood about a quarter mile to the left, and straight out from it a ridging
peak that was sending a slick, black wall tapering in my direction, chased by a
zippering fold of crystal and white. It was a perfect left—I couldn't tell how big—
but it had to be a quarter mile from where it peaked to where it peeled past me,
and then it kept curling perfectly for another couple hundred yards.

It was the most perfect wave I'd ever seen in California. It looked just like
J-Bay, but a left. And way out, tapering off south of the rivermouth, there looked
to be a comparable right. I had to go see.

Yes, the right was perfect too—at least a quarter mile long over manicured
cobble—but I wasn't thinking about that at the moment. It was the shark that
got my attention—a huge, massive great white, over twenty feet long and I
couldn't tell you how heavy—a thousand pounds? Two?—but lightened by half,
because it was the bite out of the shark that made my jaw hang and my eyes
strain, unblinking. A single grisly arc of missing flesh and muscle and cartilage
had left as much of the shark missing as there, pressed by sudden gravity, against
the dark sand near the rivermouth. The dead shark seemed almost relieved to
be safely out of the water, I thought, as I paced off the diameter of the bite at a
full eleven feet.

"Killer whale," I told myself, knowing already it couldn't be true. The bite
of the largest orca might be at most six feet across. Then maybe this was several
bites, I thought, knowing this too was impossible, since a wider, concentric
grasping bite had left hundreds of triangular-shaped wounds in the thick skin
surrounding the eviscerating bite. In fact, I knew of nothing ever seen or heard
that could take a bite of this size, unless it was some new order of oceanic monster, like a hundred-foot-long shark.

Still, I was tempted.

I had to have a look around. A back door led to a garden room and into the
kitchen. A big stove stood there, draped in dust, cupboards with the doors off, a
sink and a window with a view away to the north towards Cape Mendocino. It

appeared no one was home. Somebody had opened the gate, but they weren't in here.

On the second floor were bedrooms and a single bathroom in the common hallway. At the end of the hallway, with the light streaming through from the southeast, was a curving wooden staircase that led up into a third-story observation room. It felt very much like the bridge of a ship; indeed, Miranda had been a ship's captain for the Portuguese in the Far East. After a few decades, he grew weary of society and deceit and took his small fortune and bet it here, on gold, then redwood timber. There used to be a huge coho run up the river, my friend from Trinidad told me.

I took a swipe at the filthy bay window with my hand, but at least half the problem was on the outside. I could see well enough, though, to see the river-mouth, and it was absolutely workin'. A solid six feet, I swear, and an offshore wind was pushing the fog back out.

For a while the beach disappeared, but then it returned, and the day got brighter, and soon it was blue and the shadows were sharp the way they are in the Northern California air. That's part of the reason Flame and Vince Lyons knew those photos were taken somewhere up here.

It was great to see the sun. I went down to the car, got an old towel and a bottle of water, and washed the window. There was a door to the outside, where there was a yard-wide walk around the observatory—I guess you could call it that, considering the dome of the ceiling and its glass skylight framing a disk of the blue heaven. What a setup!

"If this place wasn't haunted, I'd be here in a flash," I said out loud, wondering if whoever had opened the gate could hear me. Some friendly ghost of a park ranger perhaps. More likely the spirit of a lost tribe's soul. I decided to move in for a while. No way I could get a window open without breaking panes, but I could leave the door open for fresh air. And when they came to arrest me for trespassing, I'd have my story.

But they never came. I stood up there watching the sets come in out of the northwest, hit the defining topography of the approaching land, and collect into a ridgeback of focusing peaks. As near as I could tell, that topography was as perfect as the Delta of Venus, and I started to feel like I had to have it. So I sat up there with the waves and the shark and the thing that killed the shark—these are the thoughts in my mind—and the gate, and the other gates, and the surfboard . . . Well, I could go on and on with this stuff, right? But they never came.

It would be six feet for a couple of hours, then four feet for a couple, then three for a while, then back up to four. The wind went a little sideshore. The sun baked. The waves peeled. The flies were on the shark like an aura. Baby seals stayed shallow and close in at the rivermouth. The waves peeled. It was seductive.

I stood on the enormous white backbone of a Doug fir and watched and watched. The waves peeled. The seals, the shark, the flies. So seductive. The seals, the shark, the flies, and the gate and the signs and the other gates and the sign TRESPASSERS WILL BE EATEN!

"Shit!" I thought. "I must be on Candid Camera." And the waves peeled. Back up to six feet, then eight for a couple of hours, then back to six. So seductive.

I walked up towards the Cape and saw a long righthander pouring down the beach at me, smoke pouring out of each barrel. It was absurd. I watched, and it just kept pumping.

On the third morning it jumped to ten, then twelve feet. The faces were deep blue, and the whitewater was shaved-ice white, and each wave peeled across like a road map of time hanging on a line. I knew a good thing when I saw it.

I'd eaten almost all my food, and I had no appetite for shark, especially old shark. I had to get going. I had an energy bar, some coffee, and some cheese, and I was out of water.

It was now or never. Nobody came. I saw nobody, there was a huge shark on the beach with an even huger bite out of it, somebody was watching me, and my time was limited, unless I wanted to drive out and back in again, which was a possibility I didn't want to consider. So it was now or never. Put on the wetsuit or turn the key.

I put on the wetsuit. What else could I do? I had no story; there was nobody to talk to, nobody to watch surf, nothing to say except "weird place." That and some stuff about the waves. I had no story if I didn't paddle out, so I paddled out.

There was no point waiting for a lull since there were none, so I was prepared for serial duck-diving. I'd try it as long as I could, and then I'd go for water and something to eat. I couldn't imagine coming back somehow, despite the wave. The road made it feel like a once in a while deal.

The current at the rivermouth was brisker than I expected. I jumped in where it cut through the beach and I rode a stream through the bobbing heads of juvenile seals and straight out into the breaking waves. I duck-dived and the current pushed me out despite the wave pushing me in. Three ducks and I was outside, involved in a perfect five-foot session. My only worry was, would the next wave, which was right there, get to me before a shark. I tried to think small, but my dangling feet seemed to broadcast my presence. Who was I trying to fool?

Five or six strokes and I was in, backside in a sucking hollow pocket, racing towards the Miranda house, sun spanking off the window where I had stood. There was no way out till well past the house, so I straightened out and proned straight to the beach, which was white sand down to the mean high-tide line and encrusted cobble from there on out.

I walked back to the rivermouth and rode the current back out. I was drunk with my good fortune and the danger and my thirst, but I rode five or six more waves before I really noticed the fatigue setting in. I had made it back out again, duck-diving through a half-dozen broken waves then punching through a folding lip to make it out to the lineup, but before I could really catch my breath I saw the horizon welt with dark lines.

I started a steady paddle as the first wave of the set lazily lifted through the outside kelp beds, dark green and glassy, and spread a steepening wall in my direction. The thinning face was feathering as I broke through the lip, blinded with spray, clawing briefly into the air then down the back of the wave. As my eyes cleared, I saw the next wave stretched across the horizon. It looked like it had me, but it held just long enough, and I punched through the cornice once again. And again. The waves kept coming, getting larger and larger, and I just made it over each of them.

My arms and shoulders were on fire, and I was feeling lightheaded and numb. Every time I broke over a wave, there was another one outside. I was way past my second wind and my third, but I kept paddling, mechanically, flat on my board under the glare of the sun, white spots now sparking into my vision, breathing rapid and hollow, and still the waves kept coming, and the sounds of their cracking and curling overlaid the steady rumble behind me and—every once in a while, woven into the work of the sea—there was a shard of conversation . . . voices drifting through it all, coming from somewhere out in the kelp, like the music of my delirium . . . voices like spirits standing at the gates, the words fragmented, indecipherable, but forming in my hallucinating consciousness a recurring phrase: "TRESPASSERS WILL BE EATEN!"

"I am no trespasser," I gasped. "I am no trespasser." Vaguely, I thought I would wake up soon in some hospital bed, muttering "I am no trespasser" over and over while the doc tried to slap me back to consciousness—"Wake up, Austen! Get hold of yourself, man!" But no such luck, just another wave.

Why didn't I turn around, straighten out, take one on the back, and head in to the beach? I don't know. The waves were big now—a solid twelve feet—and I was in a kind of stupid momentum—novocaine on the brain—and the voices . . . they were right there, close by—"TRESPASSERS WILL BE EATEN! . . . TRESPASSERS WILL BE EATEN! . . . TRESPASSERS WILL BE EATEN!" And then another wave, and—there!—just ahead in the kelp, appearing briefly as a wave beyond rose through the green weed, a shape—a large fin, black not gray. A killer whale!

I froze, struggled to sit up on my board, and was lifted by the wave, and from the height of the crest I could see over the next wave and—for just a second—a cluster of black shapes—a pod of killers. Or . . . ?

Insanely, I paddled towards them . . . because of the voices . . . because I had to see . . . over the next wave and the next, and then I broke over the top of a final dark wall, my eyes blinded, grimacing, dry heaving, expecting . . . and I blinked back my vision and took in the apparition—surfers! A dozen or so, sitting out here at the edge of the kelp forest.

"You made it, man!" one of them said.

"Welcome," said another.

They were all in full rubber and looked cheerful as hell. I was bewildered and barking from the pain in my lungs as I threw back my head and gathered what was left of my wits. The set that had gone on for so long had now stopped completely; the ocean was like a lake.

"Here y'go," one of the surfers said, tossing me a bota bag. It was cold, fresh water.

"What . . . ?" I started, gasping after a long drink.

"You made it," someone repeated.

"You mean I'm dead, and this is heaven?" I asked, gesturing to indicate this place we were in.

"You're not dead, my friend," said a surfer. "You just made it outside."

"Outside," I repeated.

"Outside," he agreed.

"And before?" I asked him.

"Inside," he answered.

"Inside," I repeated.

"The Lost Coast," he said. "You found it. Same as we all did."

"Set," someone said, and we all turned and stroked out a ways. One after another, the surfers paddled into the waves, sometimes in twos and threes, until one surfer and I remained, and we caught the last wave.

I was surprised how close the beach was. I'd been paddling for hours it seemed, but the ride was only a perfect hundred yards or so, then we straightened off and rode rail to rail to the beach.

Beyond that I can't tell you much. Let's just say it has to do with local rites of initiation. We stood around a driftwood fire and ate clams and abalone and watched an occasional set come through—nothing like before, but perfect in its own way—peeling from the rivermouth with a plunging crack and roar as the fog moved back onshore with the afternoon breeze. After a while, it was so thick I could only see the surfer closest to me, so we headed back up towards the Miranda house. He seemed to know the way, although I couldn't see a thing. I felt the soft sand give way to the firm powder of dirt road, and then the Trooper was right there in front of me.

"Hey!" I called out. "Bro!" There was no answer, and I don't think I expected one.

I still had a hunk of cheese and some coffee beans in the house, so I went around to the back door, but it was padlocked. I looked into the garden room and the kitchen beyond, and I could see the big stove draped in dust. I had been there; it was all so familiar.

"Can I help you?"

I started and turned. It was a park ranger. He wore a sidearm, a smoky hat, a badge, and a big brown mustache.

"I left something inside."

"Inside?" he said, stepping forward and giving the padlock a good shake. "When? I don't think so."

It was an easy drive out—15 curving miles up the river valley and over the crest, back into the sunshine and down into the redwoods. At the Miranda gate, another park ranger saluted me and opened the gate.

I was hungry as hell, but I turned right instead of going straight to food. I ran along the perimeter of the state land and found the dirt road that ran through the manzanita, took it about ten miles south, but I never did find the opening and the gate, and I finally gave up.

By the time I got to Eureka, it was raining again, and when I pulled off at Trinidad it was a deluge. I had coffee with my friend in the small cabin of his fishing boat, parked there in the harbor. When I told him my story, he laughed.

"You got lost," he said. "I told you not to go there, and I told you not to surf there. The place is dangerous. Forget the sharks, you can get lost."

"What do you mean, lost? Have you been down there?"

"People get lost, that's all," he said. "A lot of surfers. They don't call it the Lost Coast for nothing, y'know."

"Well," I told him, "it won't stay lost forever."

"It could," he said. "I wouldn't write about it, if I were you."

"Why?"

That was when he dropped the single transparency on the table next to my empty coffee mug. I held it up to the gray light of the window. It was a man standing on a huge white drift log looking out at a stacked set. It looked a lot like me.

"It looks a lot like me," I said, and at that he began to laugh hysterically.

"Right, right! I told you, you got lost."

The drive back looked to be another descent into Northwet hell, but north of Seaside the sky unexpectedly opened, and by the time I'd crossed the Columbia and rolled past Westport, it was sunny and warm and I had a Wilco CD whipping my spirits back into shape.

There was a solid swell pushing up the strait when I got home, but I wasn't feeling compelled, just tired. I put some water on to boil and fired up the computer to check e-mail. There were fifty-seven, of which one was interesting:

From: Stacey McMullen <StaceyM@hotdogger.com>
To: Zeke Austen <tubular@pacrim.com>
Subject: Call now!!!
Date: Tue, 17 Feb 1999 11:04:12 -0800

Hey Zeke,

No answer on your phone & message machine didn't come on, so hope you're okay. Received surfboard here at office (no return address or sender's name). Looked chomped in half by shark. It says "TK for Zeke" on the tail, and it's a 7-4, so I assume it's yours. Perhaps be better for all concerned if Lost Coast stayed lost. Call immediately when you get this, okay? Concerned . . .

—Stacey

So I wrote the story anyway, but I don't think they'll run it. Who'd believe it? I probably wouldn't myself except for this single slide. For all those guys down at the mag know, it's lost.

This story first appeared in the October 1999 edition of Surfing *magazine.*